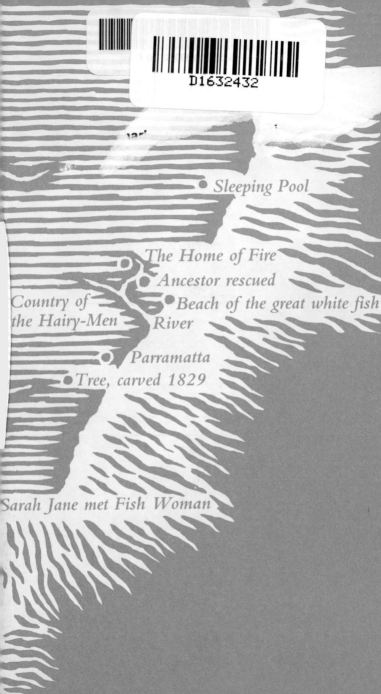

Sleeping Pool

The Home of Fire

Ancestor rescued

Country of
the Hairy-Men

Beach of the great white fish

River

Parramatta

Tree, carved 1829

Sarah Jane met Fish Woman

SHADOWS
OF TIME

A Mark Macleod Book
an imprint of
Random House Australia Pty Ltd
20 Alfred Street, Milsons Point NSW 2061

Sydney New York Toronto
London Auckland Johannesburg
and agencies throughout the world

First published in 1994
Copyright © Patricia Wrightson 1994

National Library of Australia
Cataloguing-in-Publication Data:

Wrightson, Patricia, 1921- .
  Shadows of Time.

  ISBN 0 09 182950 X.

  I. Title.

A823.3

Cover photograph by Reece Scannell.
Cover design by Wayne Harris.
Typeset by Asset Typesetting Pty Ltd, Sydney.
Printed in Australian Print Group, Victoria.
Production by Vantage Graphics, Sydney.

SHADOWS
OF TIME

Patricia Wrightson

A Mark Macleod Book
RANDOM HOUSE
AUSTRALIA

Author's Note

The shape-changing spirit in this story, the Magooya, is not an authentic figure from the folklore of Australia. It has been invented by the author, she hopes with the traditional feel of the authentic.

The Magooya

1

*I*t was in the year 1798 that the boy came running to the Hill of Fire. He was small, about eight years old, naked and brown skinned like the men who were hunting him. He had no one to whom he could run since his grandfather was dead, and no safe place to go since he belonged to no country. He ran like a small, scared animal: up from the river under dark casuarina trees, in among great, grey gum trees on the flat, making for a hill under the wall of mountains. In this country a hill would have rocks, with perhaps a cleft into which a small boy could squirm away from spears.

The men followed, grim and silent. They hunted him because his grandfather the Clever Man was now dead, and because he had no rights in their country, but most of all because he had devil's eyes. When they saw him draw near the hill they grew angry and ran faster, shouting warnings and threats.

The boy leapt on, driven by the shouts. He scrambled up the slope of the hill through long, coarse grass, searching for outcrops of rock. The shouts grew more distant: the men had fallen back. He was so glad that it did not seem strange. He scuttled like a spider around the hill to its northern slope — and was suddenly still. Now he knew where he was, and why the men shouted and fell back. Running for his life, he had blundered into a terrible place, a forbidden place. Now he was truly lost.

The hill was burning. Drifts of smoke rose out of it. There were rocks: they plunged down in great slabs where fire had eaten the ground from under them. They were black, or a sharp and shining yellow, just as his grandfather had said. He could smell the dangerous breath of fire, and see the track it had burnt long ago on its way down into the hill. He should not have seen these things, for this was the secret, sacred home of fire.

Now he would surely be killed. He waited helplessly for fire to leap out and grab him. Thick smoke rolled out of the heat-cracked soil, slow and menacing. The boy's nerve broke. He went running into the smoke, throwing himself on the hot, cracked ground, sobbing his surrender to fire. 'All right, take me. I've got devil's eyes and I know devil's talk. Take me.'

Nothing happened. Only the smoke leaned heavily north and drifted higher; and below, the men sang a solemn chant. Out of a great crack in the earth rose the breath of fire, forcing the boy to roll near. Choking, he looked deep into the crack.

At first it was only dark, and then it glowed a dull red. He could not look away. There was a face, glowing red, that looked at him with golden eyes. It was old and stern like his grandfather's face, and the boy cried out in a child's fear and sorrow. Then the smoke billowed up, and his eyes and lungs ached, and he rolled aside for air.

The men heard his cry, and stamped their feet and sang to the spirit of the fire. The boy lay still and waited: while his throat burnt; while the sun moved over the sky, and the smoke rolled up or died away; while evening filled the hollows and the men went home. Nothing happened. And quite suddenly the waiting wore out, and the boy knew that nothing would happen. He simply stood up and walked away.

His body was smeared with the sharp and shining yellow of the rocks. He shivered at that, and ran down into the river and scrubbed it away with handfuls of wet sand. But one mark, on his arm above the elbow, would not scrub away: a golden mark like a leaping flame. When he had scrubbed it till the place was sore, he gave in and would not look at it again.

He drank, and gathered shoots and berries to eat. Then he built a heap of dead leaves like a brush-turkey's nest and burrowed into it. He needed fire for warmth, and to guard against the spirits of night, but he could not make one. Today he had looked into the golden eyes of fire, and he was afraid.

In the warmth of the leaves he slept. Night-things came nosing after him: first the Magooya. It had many shapes, but tonight it was taller than trees and thinner than starlight, with pale, goggling eyes peering down. It saw the Hairy-Man and his woman hunting, and warned them off with sharp, explosive sounds: *crack! crack!* The boy heard it in his sleep, and stirred; but his leaf-nest was deep, and the trees netted it in moon-shadows, the Hairy Ones did not find him.

Far away east, at the white men's settlement of Parramatta, the convicts were sleeping too. They were locked away in the huts they had built, sleeping in irons instead of leaves, but they slept well because of hard work and a little rum. In the barracks built by convicts, candles still smoked where a few soldiers played cards or sang insulting songs about their officers. The officers were safely at home in neat cottages that the convicts had built, and by now the cottages were dark. Only Captain Allen's kitchen window had a glimmer of light, where Mistress Allen's scullery maid Tranter was running away.

Sarah Jane Tranter was eleven years old. She knew she was lucky to be Mistress Allen's scullery maid, for Cook and the Reverend Jenkins often told her so. Both her parents were dead, killed in the useless flurry of a bolting horse; she had been left alone, a young female orphan in a convict settlement on the wrong side of the world. Without the Reverend Jenkins's help she would have had nowhere to turn.

She tried to deserve the good name he had given her, and to be honest and industrious as he and Cook advised; for she knew they were right, and her good name was her greatest treasure. That was why she was running away, with half a loaf and the rest of the salt mutton stolen from Mistress Allen's kitchen. She had to preserve her good name.

She had not minded the work. She had scrubbed the front step in the dark of morning while the house was asleep, and cleaned the grate and laid the fire for Cook, and been proud to do it. She had pumiced the stains off the knife blades till they cut her fingers, and scoured the pots till her hands were raw. She had not minded being tidied away in the broom cupboard when the mistress came; for a scullery maid couldn't always stay neat, but a mistress should always see her kitchen neat. That, like the work, was only right. Sarah Jane would have gone on doing all of it gladly if it hadn't been for the gravy boat.

It was the best gravy boat, all lilac and gold. Sarah Jane was never allowed to touch it. She was scrubbing burnt pots at the tub when she heard the crash and turned to look. There it was, in pieces on the floor, and no one else in the kitchen but Cook. Sarah Jane wanted to cry because Cook was in such trouble. Then she caught a glance from under Cook's brows, and turned quietly back to the tub.

'Sweep it up, Tranter,' said Cook in a dangerous calm. She was a convict woman, and fiercely respectable.

Slowly and unwillingly, Sarah Jane swept up the gravy boat. She didn't want to touch it. She wanted to keep her good name, but Cook had been keeping hers much longer and was probably better at it. Sarah Jane behaved like a mouse until bedtime, and said goodnight to Cook's back while it was bent over the fire. Then, while the back was still turned, she tidied herself away quietly into the broom cupboard.

When the house was still she crept out. She lit a candle-end from the banked-down fire, tied the half loaf and the salt mutton into a kitchen cloth, unbolted the back door, blew out the candle, and slipped away towards the river. She had only the clothes she wore: the shift and petticoat under the long drab dress, the canvas apron over it, her yarn stockings and strong boots and her maid's calico cap; all, like the bread and mutton, provided by Captain Allen through the favour of Mistress Allen. She felt guilty, but only about the unbolted back door.

She knew she must not be caught by the sojers, to bring disgrace on her parents and the Reverend Jenkins. Apart from that, her only plan was to reach the sea. She could not remember it; she had been too small when her father, the ship's carpenter, came ashore to work in the settlement. But all her father's stories had been about the sea, and its breakers roared in Sarah Jane's dreams. The sea had fish and shellfish and warm, sunny sand. She knew she could live by it if only she could find it.

From Parramatta the only road led to Sydney Town: a wild place, not safe for a young female orphan. Rough tracks led to tiny farms torn out of dense forest; no one there wanted orphans. Everywhere else was the vast and silent bush: vine-tangled, dim, full of leeches and serpents and savages. Explorers went into it trim and brave and well supplied, and came out looking as if the cat had been at them. Sarah Jane must go through it to reach the sea, and if they found her dead it would serve Cook right.

At least she had grown up in this settlement, playing with the children of convicts and learning to run from man and dog. She knew where the men were drinking and where the dogs were tied, and the hidden places where couples might lurk. Slipping through moon-shadows past houses and barracks and huts, she found the stream and followed it north.

The stream was a kind of road through the bush: others might use it, who also wanted to keep away from people and dogs. She crept north under its bank until she needed to sleep, then struck bravely into the towering dark. When she felt the trampling of dry bark under her boots she curled up on it, tucked her bundle under her apron, and fell asleep.

In the morning she was lost. She wandered in the bush for three days before the dark skinned people found her.

They were not greatly surprised, for this was their country; in their endless journeys through it, following the seasons and the food, they had observed the white skinned race for years. Some of them had eaten white men's tucker and knew some of their words. They had saved and fed those who were lost, or who ran off with chains on their legs. This one was a young female; they knew she should be taught a little by the brown women and married off to a responsible man. But they were cautious.

The white men had strange moods and fearful weapons. The young white female had a temper: she had filled her lungs to scream. If they took her with them, she might escape and complain to the white men of being carried off; if they did not, they might be blamed for leaving her to die. It was not their business, but either way it might cause them trouble. They talked it over in rumbling words and decided that the young white female should choose for herself.

Sarah Jane too had seen brown people before, but only in the safety of the settlement and usually wearing more than mud and fat and a little string. She kept her lungs filled for screaming — but she had spent three days alone in the scrub. She had one scrap of bread and less than half the mutton, and her only water had come from marshy pools. When the dark people turned away, her heart sank. Then two of the children slid glances at her and giggled. Sarah Jane was herself a child; she could read a glance and a giggle. She followed the brown people.

She followed them for days. They watched over her but left her to herself. She learnt to see their unmarked roads, to help gather roots and berries and caterpillars, to sleep under a bark shelter near a fire. She offered the women what food she gathered, and was given a share when it was cooked. She listened with longing to their tumbling words and laughter; but she never, for one moment, thought of staying with them. A strange, new feeling was growing inside her and she did not know that it was freedom. She only knew she was Sarah Jane Tranter and she was going to the sea. And there came a night when, waking in deep silence, she felt in her ears a rhythm like a far-off giant breathing and thought it might be the sound of the sea.

She knew what to do when she reached it, to be rid of the brown people. It was easy: she would turn herself into a devil, as the son of a convict had taught her years ago. That always upset people, and while they were upset she would slip away. She waited for days till the moment came, while the far-off breathing grew into a wordless crying and the tall, damp forest became banksia and heath; until at last the people stood on a high, rocky place that fell down into marshes.

There were treetops at her feet. Sarah Jane looked over them. Beyond the marshes lay a white beach, and a rocky point where waves leapt and sprang, and a flat, sparkling blue that reached away to the sky; and she shouted,

'The sea!'

All the brown people looked at her and smiled. She could not waste a chance like that. Quickly she put a thumb in each corner of her mouth, a forefinger under each eye, and squeezed up her cheeks. Now she had a distorted, grinning face with red-rimmed eyes dreadfully staring; no one could see it without a shudder.

The women and children shrieked like magpies. The men stepped back and waved their spears. And Sarah Jane Tranter jumped over the cliff.

She thought she might be killed, but the land caught her in a net of shrubs and she was only bruised and scratched. The cliffs above were hollowed into caves; in front were steep slopes of scrub; to the right ran the dark line of a ravine. Sarah Jane hurled a stone into the ravine and crept off the other way under the cliffs. No one came after her. Perhaps they really thought she was a devil, or perhaps they were only glad to be rid of her.

She did not reach the sea that day. When she had climbed painfully down through the scrub she had still to find a way round the marsh. She slept by a stream that flowed strongly inland, and was worried by this until she remembered tides. With her new bushcraft, she drank from the broken stem of a vine and ate a few seeds and some honey from bottlebrush flowers, and was still hungry but very pleased with herself.

Distant sandhills hid the sea, but she heard it all night in her sleep. It spoke like God: one single word too large and simple to be heard. In the morning the tide was low and the stream trickled over wet sand. Sarah Jane walked down it to the sea, carrying her boots and stockings.

There were no fish or shellfish on the beach. 'They'll be on rocks,' she reminded herself, and set off towards the headland. It was a long way, but she walked at the edge of the sand where the sea kept snatching at her feet and letting them go; and she came under a high cliff to a broad stretch of rock, pitted with pools.

The sea made a thundering spray all around, but sent only threads of water over the rock and into the pools. There were crowds of shellfish, like pointed caps or twisted turbans, all stuck fast to the rocks. Sarah Jane used a pebble for a hammer. Hungry as she was, she thought crushed shellfish were a nasty mess though very likely nicer cooked. She had eaten several when a silence of the sea made her look up.

The sea was building an enormous wave. Its curled white crest rode against the sky, its green-and-purple underside leaned over the ledge, and none of her father's stories had told of anything like it. Sarah Jane dropped her pebble, snatched at her skirts and raced for the cliff. There was a smashing *boom!* and a roaring and churning of water, and boiling white foam rushing at her ankles as she ran. She thought the seaward rocks must have been smashed away.

But when she turned, pressed back against the cliff, it was all the same as before. There were only wet shells under the cliff, and a finger of spray on her face, and sleek water running away down the ledge, and pools spilling over and a great white fish stranded, flapping on rock.

Sarah Jane was still hungry, and there at last was the fish, big enough for a family. It flapped and slithered; the next wave would take it back into the sea. She rushed to it, shoved it into a deep pool and darted back to watch for the next wave.

It was only the usual explosion of foam along the ledge. Her father had said that a seventh wave was always bigger: she stayed under the cliff while she counted, but the sea did not build another mountain. When she ventured down to the rockpool, the fish was gone. It had escaped.

Sarah Jane was relieved, for she could not fancy biting anything so large and white. Her eye caught a glint on the sand in the pool;

something shone between ripple-shadows. Curious, she knelt on the rock and fished it out: a broad band of silver, a ring. Wondering, she slipped it on her finger. How could there be a ring where only savages came?

'It's off some drowned sailor,' she thought, and shivered, and quickly tried to pull it off. But the ring, which had slipped on so easily, could not in any way be made to come off.

2

The brown skinned boy slipped away from the Hill of Fire, in case the men came back or fire itself came after him. He went by the quickest way: down the river, south and east out of that country. But it seemed to him that some spirit went with him.

Now again, he dared to guard his camp with fire, yet night after night there were strange noises. They rang out sharp and clear, from the forest around or the air above. He had learnt about spirits from his grandfather the Clever Man, and this one sounded like a Magooya. The boy hoped it would fall behind, for a spirit belongs to its own country as a man does. But the river took him out of the hills, into the wet, green forests of the coastal plain, and still the spirit noises went with him.

Soon he was near a camp of the white men. He was not afraid, for his grandfather had often taken him among them; but he did not want to meet any men, white or brown. He only wanted to stay alive and free, to travel the country as his people had always done. Yet when he came on the track of a white man in the coastal scrub, he followed it. It was safer to find the man than to be found by him.

This was the track of a man with a chain on his leg; lost, for he wandered aimlessly; thirsty, for he chewed leaves and spat them out; weary, for he sat down heavily and often. At last, crouching behind ferns, the boy saw him.

He sat slumped against a tea-tree, head

bowed, eyes closed. His face, behind its shaggy beard, was burnt and cracked from the sun and his lips were swollen. He wore a canvas frock and trousers, and a broken chain on one ankle. The boy considered. *G27713*

This was a runaway convict, afraid of the wet, green forest and afraid of the soldiers. It would be easy to creep away unseen, but the man would still be wandering, lost and dangerous. It would be easy to give him a drink from the water-vine looping over his head, but he might easily grab a small boy who was so useful. There was another plan that might be safer. The boy stepped forward.

'Good day,' he called. 'You want water?'

The convict jerked away and stared about. 'Eh?' he mumbled, and saw the boy and lunged. The boy stepped back.

'Water's near,' he said. 'You come.'

The man lumbered to his feet. It was easy to stay ahead and draw him on, not so easy to find a path he could follow. They came to squelchy ground under paperbark trees. The man fell on his knees and pressed cupped hands into the mud.

'No!' cried the boy. 'Bad water, this! Good water is near!' He tugged at the man's frock to draw him on.

The convict swiped at him, sucked in wet silt and rotting leaves, spat, sucked again, and at last lurched to his feet. The boy darted on between paperbarks, finding the firmest ground for the man to follow. 'Here!' he cried, lifting and parting the weeping branches of tea-tree.

The convict saw the river, dark and mysterious under boughs, looped over by vines. He stumbled down the low bank, fell on his knees to drink, and sank on wet gravel with his feet in the water. 'Praise be to heaven,' he croaked, 'I've discovered a river.'

He drank again, and splashed water over his burnt and bearded face. The boy moved back a little, watching. He had learnt from his grandfather how this scene should go.

'Ah!' cried the convict, his voice stronger. 'I

can go back any day I like. They'll never give the lash to a man that's discovered a river.' He gazed with dreaming, bloodshot eyes. 'I'll be known for it, like that Tench. They'll name it for me, likely.'

The boy nodded, backing away; in a moment he would vanish through the swamp ... But in that moment a shrill young voice shouted, 'Shame!'

The convict and the boy both stared and stared. A small figure stood on the bank lower down. It clutched a handful of muddy skirt in one hand, a bundle of stockings and scratched boots in the other, and wore a mob-cap on its tousled head.

'You never did discover this river!' shouted Sarah Jane Tranter. 'The boy showed you! Shame!'

'Wa!' muttered the boy in disgust; for the convict had lumbered dangerously to his feet, his bright hopes threatened and his face a deeper red.

'It's not right!' shouted Sarah Jane.

'Currying favour with the nobs, doing a poor, ignorant savage out of his rights! I'll not stand by —'

Nor did she, for the boy reached her just as the convict lunged. He clamped a brown hand over her mouth, locked an arm through her elbow and yanked her off among the paper-barks. 'Do you want to be killed?' he hissed in her ear. 'Run, now!'

Sarah Jane was so astonished that she did what she was told. Behind them the convict blundered and squelched in the swamp, but he was weak and exhausted, and anxious not to lose his river. Soon he told himself it was right-down strange what hunger could do to a man: he could have sworn to a young, white, female person — as if any such could be here in the wild bush. He went back to sit with his feet in the river and to dream of a nice little grant of land at Rose Hill, or whatever heathen name they gave it now.

By that time the brown boy and the white girl were deep in the scrub, standing defiantly face to face. Sarah Jane had a word or two to say as soon as she had her breath back, but the boy had breath already.

'Why did you do *that*?' he demanded, glowering. 'You want your neck twisted like a bird's?'

'You should stand up for yourself,' cried Sarah Jane, for the convict had reminded her of Cook. 'It was you found the river. That bolter took your rights.'

'I don't want rights. I want to stay alive. And I found nothing; the river is always there. White men walk and walk, and by and by they see a river, or might be a hill. Then they are big men with big stomachs. Why? They only walked and looked. They didn't make the river or the hill. It was there.'

'Fiddle-faddle!' cried Sarah Jane. Then she saw that the boy had blue eyes, oddly vivid in his dark face. And he spoke English; and he was near her age and not a bolter. She said meekly, 'There, now. I never thought of that.'

'Where are your people?' he asked severely.

Sarah Jane gave him a friendly smile. 'Where are yours?'

The boy frowned. He was wearing a string belt with a small wooden club and an English knife tucked into it. 'Where are you going?'

'As to that,' said Sarah Jane, 'it's not quite decided. There's no hurry. Were you thinking of going south?'

He frowned again and would not answer; but she had taken his part, wanted or not, and certain things were right. 'You have food?' he asked sulkily.

Sarah Jane laughed. 'What a thing to say, when you're standing on one of those vines with roots! Not that they're nice raw, no more than fish. There's food enough, if only I'd brought flint and steel to cook it.'

He snorted. 'Flint and what-else! You cook with fire!'

'But I can't make it without flint and steel.'

'Dig the roots, then,' said the boy. And while Sarah Jane broke a sharp green stick and dug up four good roots, he found a large white fungus and wood for a fire. It was damp, like everything else in the scrub, but he made a fire quickly by pushing a stick through the fungus and twirling it. Sarah Jane thought it was almost as handy as the flint and steel, the tinder, the dry matchstick and the candle-end by which fire was made in Mistress Allen's kitchen.

'Don't you carry a firestick?' she asked, for the brown women had done this in order to save the work of making fire.

The boy was converting damp wood into red coals. He said, 'Fire is easy for me,' and laid the roots in the coals.

'If you lend me your knife I'll fetch paperbark,' she offered, to show him that she knew about such things; for she had been lonely, and sometimes afraid. He gave her the knife, and she found a big paperbark tree and brought thick, soft wads of papery bark to lean against bushes and make shelters. The smell of roasting roots was delicious.

The boy drew them out to cool, and the

children ate them by the fire while the forest darkened. A tiny lizard, black with a red stripe, rustled in the dead leaves at the boy's feet. It was weeks since Sarah Jane had felt so much at home. 'Tomorrow,' she said cosily, 'we'll have cooked fish.'

He jerked his chin. 'No spear, no line. When there is time I make these things. Now a lizard is quicker.'

Sarah Jane laughed. 'Some like lizard and some don't. I shall have fish and catch them with my hands.' She saw him glower and added quickly, 'But they're nasty without a fire.'

He was not appeased, for he was sure she was bragging. He pointed with a toe at her boots and stockings, and asked rudely, 'Why do you carry those?'

'They get that muddy in the swamp.'

'They're no good, then. Why do you carry them?'

She gave him a straight look. 'My mind's not made up. I might need them later. It's right

I should use more sense than you, seeing I'm older.'

The boy sat up with a jerk. 'Older! Who says?'

'It's plain enough. I'm better grown and older in my ways.'

'You older! If I didn't have sense for both, you'd be drowned in the river by a bolter!'

She did not argue, for fear he might run off into the bush. She only put a finger to her nose, pushed it up till it lifted her lip, and looked at him cross-eyed. This maddened him into throwing a stick, and then drew him into pushing with a finger at his own nose; so she taught him to look crosseyed, though he said it was dangerous magic.

By now it was dark. They lay sheltered by paperbark screens, each feeling the presence of the other like a new tooth. Sarah Jane put on her stockings for protection against mosquitoes. The boy sometimes pushed a stick farther into the fire, and sometimes crossed his eyes and saw two fires. A koala grunted. A colony of fruit-bats screamed in some wild fig. Suddenly, sharp and near, came an explosive *crack*!

It jerked Sarah Jane upright. 'A musket?' she cried. 'Has the bolter come?' But the boy stared up into treetops; he was waving a fire-stick and calling in strange, rumbling words. Sarah Jane looked too: dark boughs with a glitter of stars, and a shape that moved between them. It was some big thing with sharp, red eyes.

'Shout! Make a noise!' cried the boy, and went on calling his strange, rumbling words.

Sarah Jane began to shriek. 'Yow! Yoo-hoo! Parramatta! Gravy boat!' she hurled a stone at the dark thing. Its red eyes slid aside with a great, slow beating of wings. 'Brandy! Bull-ants!' shrieked Sarah Jane.

The boy arched his hands over the fire, and tall, yellow flames went leaping high. The dark thing swooped over them in a windy whirling of sparks, and slid away. The yellow flames died down.

'Where is it?' whispered Sarah Jane. She was shaking.

'Gone,' said the boy. He began to take the fire apart, rebuilding it into two small fires, one to each shelter.

'What was it, then, for mercy's sake?'

'Some kind of devil. A Magooya, might be. It makes that sort of noise.'

'Why did it pick on us? What harm did we do?'

He shrugged. 'No harm. It's following me.' And he told about coming from the Hill of Fire, and how the noise of the Magooya had travelled with him.

'Well!' cried Sarah Jane. 'It's no wonder if you're a bit crotchety! I call that a right-down nasty thing! It needs two.' And since there were two, and the fire was a comfort, and this was the first time she had ever had a fire of her own, she curled up in her shelter again.

The boy returned to his. Two tiny fires grew dim, under dark, ragged branches that had caught a star or two. 'In a while,' said the boy off-handedly, 'might be I go south.'

'There, now. And no hurry.'

'I saw that. You were going north.'

'Fiddle-faddle,' said Sarah Jane.

In the morning the boy buried the fires and scattered leaf-litter over the place. Sarah Jane rolled up the paperbark and tied it with her stockings, for it was soft and warm, and light to carry, and there might not be another tree. She looked at her boots: once she had scarcely worn boots at all, and her feet were toughening up again nicely. She pushed the boots deep into a bank of ferns.

'We'll go up the river a day or two,' said the boy. 'Might be this Magooya will go back to its country.'

In case the convict was still about, they first went a long way west. They stopped often to listen: for soldiers, or dark men with spears; for the axes of men cutting cedar, or the barking of farm dogs. Whenever the boy warned Sarah Jane to be quiet, she nodded seriously and went on telling him about her parents and the

Reverend Jenkins; about Captain Allen's house, and Cook and the gravy boat, and running away. He seemed to understand it all.

'What's your name?' she asked; for she had told him hers, and once or twice he had called her S'Jane.

'Might be I'll tell you one day,' he said distantly. 'You can call me —' and he spoke a rumbling word that Sarah Jane could not catch.

'I won't, then,' she retorted, 'if it's not your name.'

He did not know how to explain that names were secret, not even known to children. And since he could not explain he could only scowl.

'Fiddle-faddle,' said Sarah Jane quickly, in case he ran off and left her. 'I'll call you Boy. What good is a name when there's only one of each?'

They turned north to the river and it led them through a green tunnel of scrub, far beyond sounds of farms and axes. Yet Sarah

Jane saw that the boy still listened. 'There'll be no sojers so far out,' she told him kindly. 'If it's not a party exploring, there'll only be your own people.'

He jerked his head. 'Do I want to be speared?'

She stared at him. 'A little boy like you? They must be nasty savages. Why would they kill you?'

'I've got devil's eyes, haven't I?'

'No,' she said roundly. 'Your eyes are like mine.'

He nodded. 'Devil's eyes.'

Sarah Jane tilted her nose. It was red from the sun, and her skirt was torn, and broken twigs were tangled in her hair. She said proudly, 'The king has blue eyes. But I daresay a little native boy mightn't know such a thing.' He was angry and threw a stone, but he did not go off and leave her.

They camped by the river for days, listening at night for sounds of the Magooya; hoping that its longing for home had coaxed it away up the river. The solemn scrub fed them with fruit and seeds and roots and honey, and with little hopping mice to roast at their campfire. Sometimes it seemed that the boy made fire only by passing his hands over the sticks; and when he wanted to hide the smoke, he spread his hand over it and it died away. In shallow pools they found prawns and mussels, but the boy had not yet made a line for fishing.

'Look,' he taunted, as they lay on a bank above a deep pool. 'There's your fish waiting.'

Sarah Jane laughed softly. 'Little ones, young in their ways. The big ones are in the dark place under the tree roots.'

He gave her a smouldering look. 'Go on, then.'

She took off her gown and petticoat. Her apron was far away in some distant swamp and her cap lost in a lawyer-vine. She slid into the pool in shift and drawers, and her wavering, underwater shape drifted near the tree roots. There was a sudden flurry of water, and she came up wrapped in her own wet hair, gripping a large mullet by the gills.

'Who taught you to swim?' he asked jealously; for he could not always catch a swimming duck by its feet, and even his grandfather had never caught fish by hand in deep water.

Sarah Jane was exchanging wet clothes for dry while the boy killed and cleaned the fish. 'Swim?' she said. 'I can't do more than crawl about in the water. I was used to be frightened of it once — till —'

'Till when?'

'Gracious goodness, I don't know. Till I was hungry enough to eat raw fish, I daresay.'

She dried her hair by the fire while the fish cooked on hot stones. The boy turned it with a green stick. 'What made that scar on your arm?' she asked him. 'The funny yellow one. I've asked before, but you don't say.'

He said shortly, 'It's the mark of fire.' But later, when they lay in their shelters in the dark, he told of blundering into the home of fire: how he had gazed into its golden eyes and yet had lived.

'It gave you power over fire,' whispered Sarah Jane. 'You can do anything with fire. I've seen that.'

It was several nights later that Sarah Jane woke to put a fresh stick on her fire and heard tiny, secret movements near the shelters. She looked into the dark: there were shadows moving in it. Her hand jerked in fear, and the fire sent up a spurt of flame. She saw eyes, and hairy backs, and long, hairy arms. She reached a shaking hand into the boy's shelter and shook him.

'The Magooya! A lot of them!'

'Shush!' whispered the boy. 'Keep still. Don't talk.' Very quietly he reached for more sticks and built the fires to a blaze.

The flames danced and fell, the dark swept back and sprang near. The eyes were old and sad and knowing; there were short legs, and round heads on hairy shoulders. Then they were gone, vanished between the fall and leap of a flame.

'Not the Magooya,' said the boy, still softly.

'Hairy-Men. Tomorrow we go from here.'

They slept and woke, and kept the fires alight. In the morning they crossed the river and headed north.

3

'What sort of a thing is a Hairy-Man?' asked Sarah Jane.

The boy did not answer. He was worried about the northern countries ahead, where his grandfather had never taken him. He would be a stranger there, and that was dangerous: not to know the people, or the spirits, or the waters. But south and east lay the white men's camps that Sarah Jane dreaded, and west was the Hill of Fire where the men hunted him. North was the only way.

Sarah Jane nudged him with her elbow. 'What sort of a thing, then? Some kind of devil, likely.'

The boy jerked his head and rubbed his ribs. 'It's *not* a devil. It's what it says. It's hairy men that live wild in the bush.'

Sarah Jane was astonished. 'But they're *your* people that live wild in the bush, and I never saw any that was hairy!'

He turned on her. 'White devil! My people don't live wild!' And he ran off through the scrub.

Sarah Jane gathered up her ragged skirt and ran after him. 'Come back! I never said your people was Hairy-Men! I went with them and they looked after me, and none of them was wild and hairy! Come back, stupid boy!'

He did not come back, but his track was plain in the mud and leaves and she found him under a geebung tree. He was squatting amid the weeping branches, chewing the small, green fruit. Sarah Jane put her thumbs in her ears and wiggled her fingers at him.

'I *said* your people wasn't wild and hairy, and no more they are. I hope I know *that* much, when I lived with them in the bush.'

She pulled a twig of black berries from a vine that was twisted among branches of geebung.

'You know nothing,' snapped the boy.

'Indeed? Then I suppose you can tell me the king's name? And how many pennies in a pound? And how to set yeast —?'

'I can tell you you'll die if you eat those berries! And if you don't die you'll have a bad pain.'

'Fiddle-faddle,' said Sarah Jane, tossing the berries away. 'Last time you said they were good.'

'A different vine! Different leaves! Can't you even see?'

In case he ran off again, she only said, 'I can see these,' and began to gather fallen geebungs. There were a great many of them, and it took a long time to chew a little sweet flesh from each seed, so she tore a strip from her skirt and knotted it into a bag to carry some away. They set off north again, spitting out leathery-green geebung skins and chewing the seeds.

'Are they secret, these Hairy-Men? Why

did I never hear talk of them?'

'They hide. They're different; an older kind. Most times we don't see them. Might be white people don't know they're there. They stay in hard places in the hills, and they only come down to the good places at night, to get food. We stay near the fires then, because of devils. We don't see them.'

'*They* don't mind devils, then. Do they talk?'

The boy seemed uncertain. 'Most times they're quiet … They make noises, but not like talking.'

'Will they harm us? Are they fierce?'

The boy took a handful of geebungs, frowning as he tried to work out an answer. At last he said, 'Most times they're all right if you stay quiet and don't look. Most times they keep away. Sometimes they're cheeky; might be they'll trick you, or hunt you. If they get angry they're fierce like dogs. They could tear you up.'

Sarah Jane shivered, remembering stooping

shapes in the light of flames. 'For certain they're not like people, with those little legs and their arms hanging down and no necks.'

'Might be it's how they stand,' said the boy. He slumped his shoulders, bent his knees and thrust his chin forward.

'Very near!' cried Sarah Jane, and they went on towards the north, chewing geebungs and imitating Hairy-Men.

When the green forest-light began to grow dim, the boy took an uphill slope towards ridges. He listened for sounds of a strange camp and sniffed the air for smells of cooking, but there were none. 'We'll camp here,' he said, standing among rocks down the side of a ridge.

Sarah Jane objected. 'We'll be black and blue by morning, with these rocks under us. And the water's away down there.'

'You know nothing,' said the boy, for he had not yet found the water and did not like to be told about it by a white girl. 'Hairy-Men won't come here. In the dark they'd come the easy way, down the ridge.' He began to break light, leafy branches from young trees and pack them between rocks to make beds.

Sarah Jane would not help but ran down into the forest to find the water. She could feel it: a sense of quiet or stillness that was almost like hearing a note of music.

She found the water in a hollow that the rain had washed out between lillipilli trees: a wide pool with a silver thread trickling into it. It was full of waterlilies, the folded flowers raised on their stems, the leaves floating. The juicy stems and roots that were good to eat lay under the water and Sarah Jane ran to gather them. She had just stepped between the lilli-pillies when sharp, sudden sounds rang out from the branches overhead.

Crack! Crack-crack!

Sarah Jane's heart thumped and her knees shook because she was alone with the Magooya. 'Bully!' she shouted. 'Horrible thing! Ding-a-ling! Jumble-jumble!' She could see only the pool and the trees.

Crack! Crack!

It was behind: she turned and gasped. Something was groping towards her, something like a man. It was as tall as trees, old and gaunt and haggard and white as mist; and it groped because it had no head. Sarah Jane yelled, 'Butter churn!' and rushed into the pool.

The water came only to her knees. The bad, sharp noises rang all around the pool — *crack-crack! crack! crack!* — but the terrible creature came no nearer. Then the boy was there, shouting words of power and carrying fire in his hands; and the noises stopped, and the horrible thing was gone. The boy ran into the pool. His hands were empty now.

'S'Jane! The Magooya!'

'It — didn't go back to its country.' Sarah Jane's voice wobbled and the boy looked worried. She bent down to pull some waterlily stems; she would not show that she was frightened, being older. When the boy kept looking, she probed with her toes in the mud for the thick lily-corms and pulled some up. The silver ring gleamed through the mud on her hands.

'You should carry that on a string round your neck,' said the boy. 'Might be it'll come off in the water.'

'I'll not worry,' she said sharply; but her voice had stopped wobbling, so she added, 'It won't come off, no more than your scar,' and groped in the water again.

'I'll go, then,' said the boy. 'There'll be lizards up in those rocks.' He went squelching out of the pool.

Sarah Jane thought he might be offended, after coming so quickly to help. She went on gathering stems and corms; but later, while they and the lizards cooked, she told the boy about the giant wave and the great white fish and the ring in the rockpool. He listened soberly, lifting food from the fire and putting on green leaves to keep the mosquitoes away; he would not sulk again when Sarah Jane found water or caught fish.

'What's that lizard by your foot?' she asked. 'The tiny one, see, with the red stripe? It comes to the fire.'

'A fire-lizard,' said the boy, though he did not know. The lizard was strange to him, like the rest of the country.

They talked about the Hairy-Men, who might be fiercer to children than to grown men and women. After that they talked about the Magooya.

'It's bad when there's only one,' Sarah Jane confessed. 'But it went fast when you came. I wish I knew what it wants.'

'I wish I knew what it hates,' said the boy. 'If we keep on north there'll be devils with a right to be there. Might be they'll send this one home.'

They kept north for uncounted days, and the new countries did no harm to the strangers. New rivers flowed down green tunnels of leaves, and Sarah Jane learnt to watch as the boy did for a shaken branch, a column of smoke, the bounding of a kangaroo or the sudden flight of birds. At night strange spirits came drifting round the fire.

'Don't look, S'Jane! Don't look!'

'Thank you for nothing,' said Sarah Jane with her eyes screwed tight. But the mist-women and little, evil men only looked and drifted away. Even the brown people were not to be seen. Sometimes the children came on fresh tracks, or smelled cooking, or heard voices, but they never saw the people.

This was because the brown people were also avoiding the children. Stories had come from the south of two blue-eyed devil-children who travelled together: a boy who came alive out of the secret home of fire, and a girl who turned into a devil and flew away over a cliff. Wherever the children went, the stories went ahead and the brown people were afraid. They watched for tracks and fires, and sometimes heard children's voices, and sent the news on to friends and relations.

Soon it seemed to the boy that he and S'Jane had stumbled through the wind, and were lost in the magic world that lay behind it; a world of their own, where the only dangers were snakes, or the wrong berries, or Hairy-Men, and never the danger of being hunted by your own people.

They went on between the hills and the sea, and the forests fed them on lillipilli and hibiscus and palm-shoots, seeds and roots and honey, lizards and birds and small, furry animals. The swamps gave them eggs and lily-corms and fish. They stayed in pleasant places until they wanted somewhere new — or until they heard the grunts and cries of Hairy-Men at night and the boy said, 'Don't look, S'Jane. Watch the fire.' They always moved on after that.

The days ran away like sand between their fingers. There were days of rain hissing among leaves, when, under a roof of branches, the boy's fire kept them almost dry; days of storm, when they sheltered under rocks; days when the forest tossed and cried in the wind, and the children climbed into branches to be tossed for the fun of it.

'Not *that* one, S'Jane. Can't you see it might break?'

There were hot, heavy days when Sarah Jane found a pool to play in, and cold days when they snuggled into heaps of dead leaves. Sometimes they heard the sea and Sarah Jane wanted to go to it, but the boy said there were too many people there.

'That's why I left it,' she confessed. 'That and the fish. Roots are better than fish if you've no fire.'

There were weeks of rain, when the rivers spilt over the plains and crept about in the forest. The children drifted west into hills. Bare slopes rose above the trees, and high, solemn headlands of rock watched over the land. Climbing down into a gully, the children came suddenly among a party of brown men with spears. They stood frozen, but the men cried out and ran away.

Sarah Jane's legs folded up from shock and fear; yet crouched among the ferns, she suddenly giggled. 'Why did *they* run away?'

'Devil's eyes,' snapped the boy, angry because he had forgotten to be careful. 'They'll hunt us tomorrow.' He glanced at Sarah Jane. Her blue eyes were vivid in a face as brown as his. The gown and petticoat were torn to scraps, rotting in faraway forests; now she wore the skin he had given her when he killed the wallaby. Only the silver ring was a difference between them; that and her fair, tangled hair. Sometimes she shortened the hair with his knife or a firestick, but only because it caught in twigs and vines. He had not told her that long hair was another devil-sign.

That night they camped without a fire and ate raw food, but no men hunted them. Still the boy was uneasy. He remembered that he was a stranger here; they had come so far north that the shadows fell differently.

Next day they let the ridges lead them above winding valleys, where little streams leapt down to the coastal rivers. In one day the boy's throwing-stick took four of the fat pigeons called wonga. It was a feast day.

Later they came through dim forest to rocks that soared up to the sun, with sunlit waters glinting into a pool cupped in shadow. When they played in the pool, and its water had untangled Sarah Jane's hair, they wove branches into shelters for the night. While the boy made his fire, Sarah Jane wrapped the pigeons in damp clay from the pool. At dusk they sat by the fire while the pigeons roasted in their neat clay jackets.

'The fire-lizard's come, look,' said Sarah Jane. 'What does it eat, do you know? Would it be pigeons?'

'It eats fire,' said the boy, again because he did not know. He took a stick and raked two of the pigeons from the fire, and when the cases had cooled a little the children broke them open. A wonderful smell arose.

The birds came cleanly out of the clay, leaving their feathers embedded in it. Sarah Jane had grown used to meat very lightly cooked, and ate as hungrily as the boy. Licking burnt fingers and crunching small bones, they did not hear the rustles in the dark. Two more clay-wrapped birds came from the fire before its light flickered over red-brown, hairy bodies and sober, shadowy eyes watching from the dark. The smell of roasting had drawn the Hairy-Men. They stood at the edge of the firelight, silently watching.

The boy hissed a warning, but Sarah Jane was too startled to hear. In one shocked movement she seized a pigeon in its cover of baking clay and hurled it at the Hairy-Men.

If it burnt her hand, she never knew. Perhaps it burnt a Hairy-Man. There was a howl that might have been of pain, and then a chorus of angry yelps and chatterings. The ring of hairy bodies swayed nearer. Lips snarled, white teeth shone.

'Earless!' hissed the boy. 'Run!'

'Where, then? They're all around!'

The hairy bodies surged nearer, tightening the circle. The boy arched his hands over the fire and made it leap high. Above the angry yelps and howls came another noise: *crack!*

crack! crack!

The Magooya was there. In the light of the fire loomed a monstrous, tailed beast with a blunt head swaying on a snakelike neck. It glared with its red eyes, and swept its great tail to and fro. The Hairy-Men fell back, and cried out as if they knew and feared it.

'Run now!' hissed the boy, and the children ran. The dark forest trapped them in branches and tripped them with roots and vines and tumbled them into ferns; and they heard the angry grunts and howls of the Hairy-Men still coming.

'A tree! We could climb!'

'They climb faster. They can twist trees like string.'

Sarah Jane fell over another root. 'They must do as they choose,' she panted. 'I've no more breath.'

The boy made a frightened sound, for the Hairy-Men were all around and the dark was full of strange devils. He grabbed at her. 'Get *up*, S'Jane. They're angry.'

She held his wrist and cried, 'Stop! Listen!'

The boy's head swung this way and that. 'What? Where!'

Sarah Jane could not answer. She only felt, through the ground she was sitting on, some deep, safe quiet. There was a howl from above: a Hairy-Man had climbed a rock or tree. The boy turned to run, and Sarah Jane scrambled up and cried, 'This way!'

He followed because all the ways were the same. They ran, and listened, and scrambled up a hillside with the grunts and cries of Hairy-Men below. They stood for a moment to breathe, and even the boy felt the quiet. They followed it over the hilltop and down the farther slope, and came through trees to open space. Below lay a pool.

It was locked among trees, profoundly quiet, with only the gentle singing of little frogs. The dark water caught and held the stars; they lay on it like gems, and wavered and grew still. The children gazed, caught in the quiet, and again the bright, reflected stars wavered and grew still.

'It's the water breathing,' whispered Sarah Jane. 'It's asleep. We're safe here.' The stars wavered. The water secretly rose and fell.

'Come away,' said the boy. But Sarah Jane would not come, and it was she who wore the silver ring. The frogs sang, stars shimmered, softly the water rose and fell, and Sarah Jane knelt by it and laid her hand at its edge. The water washed gently over her fingers and sank again.

The boy drew back. After a time he curled up in dead leaves under branches of lillipilli and slept. The girl lay where the sleeping water rose and touched her hand.

All night she shared its dreams. They carried her deep into caves and up into clouds, took her tumbling down waterfalls and washing in the waves of the sea, hid with her in the veins of a leaf or in secret rivers flowing under deserts. They showed her water gardens deep under the ground, where green plants swayed in water clear as glass and blind fish swam among them, and silky curtains of weed hid the bones of ancient monsters; and many other things.

In the night the Hairy-Men came, as they often came to the Sleeping Pool. They saw the children sleeping there, and stood with their long, hairy arms hanging loose and gazed with their eyes set deep among wrinkles. Then they went silently away.

When the children woke, the sun lit the treetops and cicadas sang over the pool. Sky and treetops were mirrored in it, wavering as the water rose and fell; and a fire-lizard was sunning itself on a leaf.

Sarah Jane scooped it up. It bit her finger, and she dropped it on the boy's shoulder. It scuttled down his bare back to his belt. The boy wriggled, partly from the lizard's tickling and partly from uneasiness. He knew he had no right here, for the ring was Sarah Jane's; and the high rocks of the Hairy-Men were near.

'Come *on*, S'Jane, I'm starving.'

They went east down the ridges, leaving the

heights to the Hairy-Men and gathering breakfast as they went. They played hide-and-seek, moving like shadows: the boy was hunting Sarah Jane by the rustle of leaves and the flight of a bird when he was startled by another sound.

It came ringing and echoing up from a stream below: the sound of white men's axes.

The boy's head was suddenly filled with danger. He called softly, 'S'Jane!' and she came running up the ridge because she too had heard. Before she could begin to talk, he gripped her arm and dragged her across the ridge to its farther slope.

'How did they come here?' she demanded, pulling her arm away. 'Will there be sojers and a camp?'

'Might be.'

'Fiddle-faddle. There was no talk of such a thing. It's your own people, likely.'

'Have sense, S'Jane,' snapped the boy, for they both knew the rhythmic sound of two white axemen working together.

'They'll be off some ship, then,' Sarah Jane declared. 'Bolting over the side and swimming to shore, most like.'

'With their axes hanging round their necks, might be,' he scoffed, and added, 'Ships don't come here.'

'Gracious goodness, they go everywhere in storms. I know more about ships than you, I hope. My father was off a ship.'

They camped again without a fire, and curled up in beds of dead leaves; and the boy said, 'It's time to go.'

'Go?' cried Sarah Jane. 'Go where? For what?'

'South,' said the boy. 'To bury my grandfather.'

4

Sarah Jane sat up suddenly, scattering dead leaves. 'Bury your grandfather? Why? Is he dead? How do you know?'

The boy was vexed. 'Of course he's dead. He was dead before you came.'

'But someone must have buried the poor soul? Where did you leave him?'

'In a hollow tree,' muttered the boy. Sarah Jane thought he was right to be ashamed until he added, 'I couldn't get him up in the branches. I did make the proper marks.'

Sarah Jane was upset. 'I never did hear the like! *My* mam and dad were buried very nicely before ever I went to Mistress Allen. With flowers and the Reverend Jenkins. I declare, I never could run wild in the bush like a hocus-pocus if my mam and dad weren't properly buried. It's not right!'

The boy's eyes flared. 'You don't know right! My grandfather taught me right, and I'll do what he said! My grandfather was the best man ever.'

'So were my mam and dad!' shouted Sarah Jane. She shouted because it seemed so long ago. They ate yams in sullen silence, and at last Sarah Jane muttered, 'I'm sorry about your grandfather.'

'He was old,' said the boy, drooping his proud head.

'How long should he stay in a tree, did he say?'

'Till his bones are clean. Two years, or might be three.'

'Two or three years we've been wandering?' cried Sarah Jane. 'We've not grown!'

The boy frowned uneasily at the fire. 'We've come a long way. We've got to get back, and then south.' They had come so far, and through so many countries, that he could not tell how long the way might be.

Next day they turned south, and a fire-lizard rode on the boy's knife. 'Might be the Magooya won't come,' he said.

'Might be pigs can fly,' retorted Sarah Jane. 'But I can tell you what it hates, for the pool told me. You said you wished to know.'

'I never did.'

'You did … once. It hates water.'

He said jealously, 'It hates fire too, then.'

'Fiddle-faddle. Fire quietens it, but it hates water. Water's so big, anything might fear it.'

'Not you. It's on your finger.'

Sarah Jane laughed. 'That little thing? Water's too big for that.'

They kept to the hills because the boy said it was easier than crossing the swamps and rivers of the coast. He seemed anxious, listening for axes and watching the shadows; and he would not stay in good places as they used to do. That may have been why they saw no Hairy-Men; or perhaps the Hairy-Men too listened for axes, and let the children pass.

The days went by uncounted, wet or windy, hot or cold. From high places they saw the sea shining in the east, and blue shadowed plains to the west, and bushfires leaping among forests. And on windy hilltops, and by firelight while dingoes were crying in the dark, the boy talked about his grandfather.

'He took me when I was a baby. They'd left me for the devils and dingoes; but he said my eyes were from white people, not devils, and

61

he took me away. He'd say, "You're both. Might be that's good".'

Sarah Jane nodded. 'So he taught you both.'

'He left me a year with a white man, till I knew the words. Then he took me back. He took me everywhere. He was a Clever Man. He taught me everything.'

'It was terrible for you when he died,' said Sarah Jane. She had learnt about burying laws now, and how to help a spirit find its home.

They followed the winding of the hills southward for a long time. Once they met a party of brown women who screamed and ran away; once they heard the ringing of axes. They reached a place of broken forest and rutted mud, and knew the cedar getters had been there. It drove them higher into the hills, into drier country and colder winds; and Sarah Jane untied her carry-bag so that it became a wallaby skin again, and snuggled into the fur.

The boy's club killed another small wallaby, and they camped while he cleaned its hide with stones and his knife. Sarah Jane sat in a tree and gazed over forests far below. Out of the blue haze rose a thin column of smoke: too tall for a campfire, too neat for a bushfire.

'It's a chimney,' she said, and suddenly ached for the chimney: for someone cooking in a pot and someone sitting at a table, strangers whom she would never see.

That evening, while the wallaby roasted, she climbed up again and searched the windy dark. She was looking for a tiny point of light, steady in spite of the wind: a candle. There was nothing, and the boy called her away. But she wanted to tell those strangers she was here, that she was Sarah Jane Tranter, a good scullery maid, and she never had broken the gravy boat.

Now they did see Hairy-Men again, smaller and greyer than the others, more silent, and quicker to vanish. They came to the firelight like grey, scuttling spiders, and Sarah Jane kept her eyes down as the boy did. Only once she was startled and looked up; eyes were watching and then were gone, and she felt a sort of pain. The eyes were so secret and seemed to know so much.

Days slipped by like sand through the children's fingers, and a soft powder of snow fell in the high hills. Sarah Jane was frightened, but the boy had seen snow once before. They came lower, into forest that the cedar getters had passed through; there were muddy tracks as wide as roads, and wheel ruts, and once they heard a distant crying like cattle. It made Sarah Jane uneasy, but the boy only watched the shape of the hills. He said the Magooya's country was coming near.

'Might be it'll go home this time.'

'Might be,' said Sarah Jane, mocking him; but she added, 'You've the king's English now, very near.'

He gave her a cheeky grin. 'I've the Reverend Jenkins's English. It was him that taught me.'

She stared in delight. 'Him? Why, then, we're brother and sister, very near! No wonder if we fight.'

'We fight because fire took me and water took you.'

'You must speak for yourself,' Sarah Jane retorted. '*I* never looked into anything secret. I found a ring and it won't come off. There was nothing else.'

'There was a fish.'

'Fiddle-faddle to the fish.'

'You think you know everything.'

She gave him a cross-eyed stare. 'I can't help it if I'm older.' He threw a stone and she dodged.

They found the Magooya's river running fast and deep, and turned upstream to find an easier crossing. The river had changed since they saw it last. There were tracks and churned mud all along the banks, and ragged forest where timber had been cut; and in a while there was a sound: a strong, deep sound coming down the river. The children paused to listen, and quickly hid behind hop-bushes to watch. It was a sound of men singing.

The voices faded and grew strong again,

coming round the bends of the river. They sang high or low but all in time, blending into one strong note as men's voices do. At last, as they grew stronger, a great raft came slipping round a bend of the river into view.

It was made of huge logs of cedar roped together; and on it sat the convicts who had cut the logs. They were ragged and dirty from the bush, with tangled beards and sunburnt faces. They did not look at the banks, or the current that carried the raft, or the officer who rode with them, or the overseers with their whips, or each other. They only sang: sea songs and comic songs and songs of their far-off homes, all to the same slow beat; tired men adrift on a wild river, singing themselves home.

Moved by pity, the children watched them pass, and heard their voices fade, and crossed the river in silence. They camped near the river that night, wondering what else had changed while they were away, and if there were new settlements near.

After that they travelled carefully, scrambling through scrub for fear of the white people. Twice, for safety, they camped without fire: once under dead leaves and once in nests of grass. And at last, through the swamp where they had run away from the bolter, they came back to their own first camp.

It was hard to tell the place, so hidden under new scrub, but the boy thought he had found it; and Sarah Jane, creeping through vines and ferns, came out with her own old boots. They were green with mould and twisted out of shape. She banged them against a tree and shook out a frog.

'Put them on,' said the boy.

Sarah Jane dropped them at once. 'They've gone all bent and nasty. My feet are as good as leather now.'

'Put them on,' he said urgently.

Sarah Jane sat down. She took up a boot, worked it to and fro to soften it, and wriggled her muddy foot into it. She stood up.

'Ha!' cried the boy. 'Could you walk in it?'

'I could if I could make it soft again.' She stood in one misshapen boot, a vine tied round her waist with the wallaby-skin tucked into it, and her blue eyes clouded with thought. 'How many summers and winters?' she asked.

'Not too many,' he said, grinning. 'The boot fits.'

'But how many, do you suppose!'

'Two, might be. Or three.'

'It's not natural ... I always do grow in a year ...'

'You haven't, then,' he said, still grinning.

Sarah Jane pulled off the boot and hurled both boots away into the ferns.

And still they did not count the days, for now they had to go south past settlements they no longer knew, and all the country was changed. There were rough tracks running through the scrub, worn by hoofs and wheels. They led to cottages of bark or slabs, with a goat or a cow tethered in a yard fenced by fallen trees; or they led to roads where drays were drawn by bullocks, and convicts in chain-gangs wheeled carts of broken bricks to fill the potholes, and once a coach went lurching by, filled with people strangely dressed.

Sometimes there were fine houses with grand doors and windows. Often there were barking dogs, and men in shirts or women in shawls who stared hard at the children. It was good when they found a road running west, and could follow it and hide in the scrub at its edge. It turned them west again, towards the hills; but the boy said he must go west soon, and it was the safest way round the settled country.

Sometimes it was hard to find food and dangerous to light a fire. Once they took beans and carrots from a garden at night; once, while a woman milked a cow, Sarah Jane crept into her cottage and found a piece of hard salt beef that made them both sick. Often there were streams with little fish, and quiet places in the bush where they could camp and make a fire, and it seemed like home.

'There's another fire-lizard on your belt! It must tickle, surely?'

'Of course not,' snapped the boy, embarrassed because he had not known the fire-lizard was there.

The road took them a long way, but when it began to turn north they left it and made their own way into the hills. By then only a few farms clung to the river; it was easy to slip past and easy to find good food, and soon they were safe in the hills and travelling south again.

'What's south for you?' asked the boy.

'Your grandfather, poor soul.'

He frowned. 'You never knew of him when you said south.'

So she told him about the mysterious land that soldiers and convicts spoke of, and sometimes ran away to find: a wonderful country far off in the south, where strange white people lived and there were good things for everyone. The boy said it was all dream-talk.

'Indeed,' said Sarah Jane stiffly, 'then I suppose the governor is dreaming too, for he sent men to find it. I should think the governor knows better than a little boy, seeing he stands for the king.'

'The king knows nothing. My grandfather knows more than the king.'

Sarah Jane clapped her hands to her ears and cried, 'Blah-blah!' to shut out these wicked words.

They went south with the hills, sometimes staying to play with a waterfall or an echo, or to hone the boy's worn knife or make a new digging-stick. There seemed no hurry now, since Sarah Jane's boot had fitted. The boy knew these hills well, and in time he began to look for a westward ridge. One day, perched high in a tree, he called that he had found it.

They went west along this ridge until jagged rocks stood above tree tops gashed by a stream. The boy found a way down between brave, improbable trees clinging to rock, and pride forced Sarah Jane after him. The way ended on a cliff top.

They camped in a cave and roasted little, furry rats, and next day swung on lawyer-vines down sheer stretches of rock. Sarah Jane kept her eyes tightly shut. Below there were steep slopes, and the stream running from basin to basin; and at last they came down the slopes to the broad western country where the spirit of the boy's grandfather waited.

Tensely, the boy searched for landmarks and for signs cut in trees. 'You'll be a joyful sight to his poor spirit, waiting all this time,' said Sarah Jane to encourage him.

He muttered, 'The tree's grown. The marks are old. The bones are gone.'

'Can't you find the right one, then?'

He snorted. 'It is the right one. These are my marks.'

Sarah Jane went to look. The tree had been hollowed by rot or termites and the hollow opened by fire. Above the opening was a silver-grey scar where the bark had been stripped and a pattern of deep grooves cut in the wood. The hollow was empty. Sarah Jane looked for another tree with a hollow trunk and a pattern of grooves. There was one with a smaller blaze, and axe-cuts in a pattern she could read: *C.S. 1829*.

'What does it mean?' cried Sarah Jane, feeling as if she had fallen out of the tree. 'Whatever does it mean?'

The boy wandered restlessly among trees, returning often to the first, frowning over it and wandering off again. At last he came to Sarah Jane's tree and frowned over that. He could not read the marks, but he knew their strange disorder and the sharpness of their cutting. He said briefly, 'One of your people made them,' and turned away.

'Thank you for nothing,' she retorted. 'I can read, can't I? His name started with C and S, and he came here and marked it on a tree. But why has he put these numbers, this 1829? It isn't sense!' When the boy took no notice she stamped her foot and shouted at him. 'It was 1798 and my feet were still sore when I found you with that bolter! But this says some-one was here in *1829*! It's above *thirty years*!'

His frowning eyes met hers at last. She wanted him to say, 'Have sense, S'Jane.' But he only stood fitting her worry to his, and she was more frightened than ever. She said bleakly, 'Indeed, you carry your years well. I'd never take you for an old man above thirty.'

He turned without a word and strode off into the forest. Sarah Jane slumped to the ground under the tree where someone with a good steel blade had cut his initials and the date 1829.

The South Country

1

Sarah Jane crouched alone all day, deeply afraid. In the late afternoon the boy came back. He looked the same, except that he held a stone axe and carried two dead lizards. He said, 'Come on. There are yams. I'll make a fire.' She stood up slowly and followed.

'I'm not an old man above thirty,' he said over his shoulder. 'I'm the same. So are you.'

She knew it, but the figures were cut on the tree. She said, 'It'll be eighteen hundred and twenty-nine miles, not years.'

'No, S'Jane.'

'Of course it will! It's where he came from!'

They reached a stream. The boy laid down the axe and lizards. He said, 'The trees are grown. My death-marks are old. The bones are gone. We knew already.'

'We never did! The boot fitted. How could we know!'

'We knew with another ear. We went a long way, past what my grandfather knew, and we stayed where we liked. It took a lot of time. And white men's axes, so far north. New towns. My people running away. It was all wrong.'

Sarah Jane stamped her foot. 'I never heard such a fandangle! How could we traipse about for thirty years and not grow? Answer me that!'

But the boy had lived all his life among spells and spirits and was used to them. He said, 'We've had fire and water put on us, that's magic. The people made us devils because we *are* devils.' Then he began to make a fire.

Sarah Jane shouted that he was an ignorant savage, mad as a hatter. She made her worst faces and threw stones and sobbed. He said nothing. With a dark, fierce face he made the fire and dug yams and cooked a meal and ate.

Sarah Jane ran off among trees, and only came out of the shadows at dark to slump by the fire. Her fingers, restless among dead

leaves, met a strip of bark with a grilled lizard
and baked yams. She nibbled a yam. The boy
said nothing.

Sarah Jane turned to him haughtily. '*You*
may be a devil. *I* am Sarah Jane Tranter, I'll
thank you to mind.'

He nodded. She tossed her head and
swallowed a sob.

'Where do devils go, then?'

He said, 'South. To bury my grandfather.'

The same! It was the same, like the ground
and the sky! A warm wave of comfort swept
over Sarah Jane. She took a bite of yam and
said, 'I thought you'd lost the poor soul.'

'Only his bones. His spirit's here. I have to
find another way to send it home.'

'What will you do?'

'Get help.' His eyes, looking sideways, held
sparks of reflected firelight. 'Find this magic
South Country, where you said the white
people live.'

'You said it was only dream-talk!'

'So it is, your way. It's true my grandfather's

way.' And he told her of the southmost edge of the land where the hills sprang out of the sea; the secret country of the great white spirit Loo-Errn, where no one could come without leave.

'And this Loo-Errn can help you?'

'Of course. He knows everything.'

'But how can you find him if you can't go there?'

He growled, 'I've got fire, haven't I?' She saw that he had some plan in his head, but he would not talk about it.

Sarah Jane lay awake and thought about being a devil: if magic could be put on you, it could be taken off … surely …

Next morning they left that place, and the trees cut with stone and steel. The boy wore the axe, its bent-wood handle pushed through his belt, its ground-stone head resting in the small of his back. Sarah Jane said nothing; she knew it must be his grandfather's axe, taken from some hiding place.

They climbed a peppermint gum to look

over the plains. There were patches of grassland amid the trees, and the wide-spreading tops of redgums marked the streams. Rugged hills, all dark with forest, closed around. 'I don't doubt you know where this magic country is,' called Sarah Jane from her branch.

The boy frowned. He was trying to fit hills and streams into the map in his head. But it was long ago that he had learnt it from his grandfather, and perhaps he had it wrong, or the country had changed. He said sternly, 'Of course I know. It's west past the snow country and south over the Big River.' They climbed out of the tree and set off.

The sea was far away beyond the mountains; the land stretched north and south and west beyond knowing; the plain lay wide and empty between its hills. Bushrangers hid in the dark, rough hills, but the children did not know it. Brown people walked the plain, and sometimes glimpsed the children and ran away; they knew the old stories and would not meet the blue-eyed devil-children who never grew up.

There were new barracks to the north, and convicts building a road, but the children did not go that way. There were busy explorers carving their names and dates on trees; making maps; checking up on each other; discovering new country, only to find that determined settlers had broken through the bounds of settlement and were farming there already. The upland country hid them all. Sometimes the wind carried, faint and far off, the lowing of cattle or the bleating of sheep. The children thought these were the cries of spirits.

They followed the sun west, over the plains and the rocky feet of hills, eating as they went: raspberries and apple-berries, nuts and green shoots and honey blossom. A lizard or a bandicoot was for cooking later on, along with roots, or a bird, or perhaps a young eel. The boy cooked each as he had learnt: roasted on stones, baked in mud or ashes, grilled on hot coals.

'Mind, there's a fire-lizard. Don't burn the

poor thing.'

'Move it, then,' said the boy carelessly.

'Move it yourself. It's you they like and me they bite.' But the boy did not trouble, and the tiny lizard flickered away.

When the cooking was done, and before they slept, they often built up the fire for light and warmth. Then the flames might call up a story to tell; a shivery tale from long ago, or some happening that one of them remembered. Sometimes they sang, the boy a chant about a possum hunt and Sarah Jane a sea song from her father or a love song from Cook. There were nights when shadowy creatures came drifting near the fire, curious or lost and wandering: wrinkled old men as small as children, women with horns or claws, double people joined together, shapes that had human and animal parts mixed up.

'Shut your eyes, S'Jane. Don't look.'

'Thank you for nothing,' whispered Sarah Jane with her face against her knees. But the wandering spirits only drifted away. Perhaps they would not trouble devil-children.

Day after day the children travelled west. The sun lit up white shapes in the southern sky, and only the wind could tell if they were clouds or snow. The boy watched the hills and listened to the memory of his grandfather's voice. The days went by, wet or windy, hot or cold; and one day they came through dense forest to a muddy trail trampled by hoofs. Sarah Jane dropped her digging-stick in surprise.

'Cattle, is it? And sheep, look! Where did they come from? How can there be so many?'

The boy hid his own surprise. 'There'll be farms, of course. They've had thirty years.'

'But so far away, and so many animals! There must be a lot of people keeping them. I wonder how it is we don't see them. It's like someone creeping by at night. Why do we never see them?'

'We go short ways and find what we want. Your people take it with them on horses and wagons, and then more for the horses, and more horses to carry that. They go long, slow ways. Might be they won't get there at all.'

Sarah Jane put her thumbs to her ears and wiggled her fingers at him. 'They did, then. They've made a right-down road.' She ran down to inspect the trail.

It ran north and south, stripped bare by sheep and littered with the droppings of cattle. Here a tree had been felled to make room for it, there it wandered over grassland into open forest. There were four bushrangers hidden in a thicket on the farther side, but Sarah Jane did not see them.

The bushrangers were resting themselves and their horses. When they heard children's voices speaking English, they sprang up like cats. Each man gripped his horse and his gun as they peered from the thicket.

They saw no escort of soldiers, no coach or wagon to rob; only two naked, English-speaking children alone in the empty land. They relaxed, and nodded and grinned. It would be a joke to catch these children and make them into good bushrangers.

Sarah Jane picked her way round a boggy patch. 'It's a nasty place for walking,' she called. Then she found something in the mud and pounced on it with joy: a small horn comb, fallen from some drover's pocket. The boy came to see; he did not care much for the comb but it suggested other finds. They were bent over it when the horses and yelling riders crashed out of the thicket.

The bushrangers were a terrifying sight. They had pistols stuck in their belts, and their eyes peered from under broad brimmed hats festooned with pink ribbons. Stolen brooches and pins glittered and shone on their vests. Even their bridles were hung with watches and rings.

The children screamed and raced for the forest. The horses pounded after them, lithe and sure among trees. 'Hide!' shouted the boy, but the bushrangers were too near. Sarah Jane saw a reaching arm and dodged it by hurtling round a tree. The boy leapt for a branch and hung there. And suddenly all this confusion turned into madness.

Out of the forest came a shrill horse-scream and a thunder of hoofs. The bushrangers' horses snorted and flung up heads and heels, their riders cursed and tugged at reins, and down swept a great black stallion. His head reached into the branches, his white teeth were bared, his red eyes rolled, and he screamed as he came. While the bushrangers struggled and swore, their horses smashed out of the forest and bolted along the trail. And the huge, black stallion went thundering after them.

The boy dropped from his branch and leaned against the tree. Sarah Jane found herself sitting beneath it. She said weakly, 'That Magooya. I didn't hear its proper noise.'

'We should move. It'll come back.'

'It must do as it chooses. I've no bones for moving.' She stared at her open hand. 'There's my comb, still!'

He nodded, listless from fright, and said,

'You'll want to wash the mud off. Come on, S'Jane, they'll come back.'

They crept to the nearest stream and hid under the tea-tree boughs, but neither the bushrangers nor the Magooya came back.

'That's twice it's let us be,' Sarah Jane pointed out. 'Last time it was Hairy-Men, and just as lucky this time. Those were bush-rangers, with all their wicked thieving hung on them like the washing. Dodging the sojers, I don't doubt.'

'For sure that trail's not safe,' said the boy.

Yet they followed it, from behind a screen of forest; for the hills had told the boy it was time to turn south, and the overlanders' trail took the easiest way. Twice it led them near slab-built cottages on log-fenced farms, where the cries of sheep were too real for spirits and the barking of dogs warned the children away. Sometimes they made their own way through the hills while cattle or sheep went by on the trail below. Once they hid from a party of explorers who were opening up the south.

'Why do they trouble?' cried Sarah Jane. 'With all the people and animals here already? Freemen and all, I don't doubt. Are there convicts still, do you suppose?'

'Most like,' said the boy, 'to do the work.' He was spinning a possum-fur cord to carry Sarah Jane's comb, for she often dropped it and went back to search. Sometimes she combed her wild hair by the fire at night, giving sharp little cries of pain while she fought the tangles.

'Throw it in the fire, S'Jane. It's no use to you.'

'I don't choose to be a wild savage like some.'

In time, from a hillside they looked down on a river winding like a monstrous snake. Sarah Jane brooded over it, but the boy stared south; for this was the Big River, the edge of his world. Beyond were strange countries, and at last the magic one of Loo-Errn, and the far southern sea.

'I don't know what harm can come to two who have fire and water,' said Sarah Jane, to give him courage.

'You know nothing,' said the boy, and crossed his eyes as she had taught him; but he was comforted.

They went lower down again, and lost sight of the river. Now the trail often ran through clearings, and the children let the wind take them safely past the dogs. Once they almost blundered into a herd quietly feeding, its drovers reined in at the rear, talking to a uniformed rider with pouches strapped to his saddle. To Sarah Jane the drovers, in short vests and shirtsleeves, were only half dressed; and the other man's jacket was a poor, mean thing without cape or skirts. The men called a few last words over their shoulders as they parted.

'Not in this Year of Our Lord Eighteen-forty!' shouted a drover, laughing.

'— delaying Her Majesty's mails!' called the man in uniform, heading north.

Sarah Jane stood in a daze until the boy seized her hand and dragged her away. He spoke to her, and she only stared unhearing. At last he pushed her against a tree and shouted.

'Listen, S'Jane! It doesn't *matter* about the years! We can't help it. What *difference* is this Lord Eighteen-forty? If you hadn't heard, everything would be the same.'

Sarah Jane roused herself. 'For shame! What difference, when he said *Her* Majesty! It means the king is dead, of course. They'll forget about us in England now, I shouldn't wonder. And who's this queen I never heard of?'

She mourned the king in silence all that day. The boy was silent too out of respect; he did not know the king, but he knew the need to mourn.

He carried in his head, from his grandfather, pictures and maps of many countries in this land. He was looking for the Big River near its beginning, below the snow country; for a shape of hills, and streams running in from the south, and for one small steam that would lead him to another. And one day, looking down again on the Big River, he thought he had found the place. There were huts in a clearing, and sheep penned between logs. A punt with a muddy deck was moored on the river. 'They take the sheep right over the river, look!' cried Sarah Jane.

The boy took no notice. Across the stream, a washed-out bank made a bay where a small southern river slid into the big one. The boy gazed uncertainly at that.

Sarah Jane sniffed. 'We'd do better with a proper river. That one's a right-down trickle. Will it do?'

'How do I know? We have to cross over and find out.'

They reached the river in the late afternoon. It was fresh from the mountains, cold and lively and strong, and the boy was not sure they could cross it unseen from the huts. So they waited for dusk, when the smell of cooking told them the drovers were busy indoors. Then they slipped quietly down the bank.

'I never!' whispered Sarah Jane. She stood in the water looking suddenly astonished. 'It's a fire-lizard on your axe!'

The boy shrugged. 'Must be it can swim. Come on.'

But Sarah Jane scooped the lizard into the furry lining of her wallaby-skin bag. She only muttered crossly when it bit her, and she held the bag above the water on her digging-stick.

They came ashore within the mouth of the bay, hidden by the bank. The south land faced them, and the little stream running out of it. The boy was shivering. Sarah Jane shook the fire-lizard out of her bag, and it vanished among grass roots.

'What did you worry for?' said the boy, rubbing himself warm with a handful of leaves.

'It hates water,' said Sarah Jane, still astonished.

'It can stay on land, then. There's always another one.'

'Gracious goodness!' cried Sarah Jane. 'Will you listen? I knew when I stepped in the river. It hates water. It loves fire. It likes you and bites me. It kept us from the Hairy-Men and the bushrangers. It's the same one all the time.'

'Earless!' he shouted. 'It couldn't be! The Magooya? No!'

'Did you ever see a fire-lizard before you had fire put on you? Answer me that.'

But the boy would not answer; and no fire-lizard came to their camp that night. They found green beans near the river, and wattle sticks for burning, and gum to make the river water sweet. When they had eaten, they crawled into beds of warm earth and slept close to the safety of their fires.

They followed the small stream south until it led them into swamp, then climbed across slopes to the next river. They did not see either the fire-lizard or the Magooya, though sometimes Sarah Jane thought she heard a warning *crack*. Perhaps it was a gunshot, for all this country was alive and busy.

There were rough tracks that led only to farms; there were hurrying horsemen, and slow waggons, and settlers on the move with stock, and wandering groups of brown people.

There were fires clearing new ground, and frightened kangaroos fleeing from them through smoke that turned the sunlight a dirty yellow. The white people never saw the children; the brown people saw and ran away. At night there were crowds of shifting, restless spirits.

'They're upset, must be. Don't look, S'Jane.'

The land rose gently into high country, quiet and peaceful. Ancient granite rocks rose out of it, bigger than houses. The children met the south winds, and the boy hunted for possums in hollow trees; their skins, tied together, made warm, untidy cloaks. Grey, powdery snow drifted down and melted.

In time the warm days came back. New little streams flowed south instead of north, under hedges of tall grass. One of these led to the edge of the high country, where it fell away in great cliffs to the scrub below. 'How can we ever climb *that*?' cried Sarah Jane. 'Must we go down?'

'Not here. It's easier west.'

They went west along the scarp and saw, far down, white sand and the sparkle of sea. Sarah Jane gazed in delight, but the boy looked for hills rising out of the sea. He glimpsed them through grey-green forest running gently down a ridge, and next evening they camped far down that slope, enclosed in forest. Beyond, the hidden sea whispered its one large word in the voice of God.

'You should wait for me here,' said the boy. 'There's food, and places to hide. You could go to the sea.'

'I could if I was to wait. But I shall come with you to the sea and the magic country.'

'No,' said the boy. He had saved fat from a roasted goanna and was rubbing it into his face and body. 'You can't come to Loo-Errn's country. You're a woman.'

'When I've come all this way for your grandfather!' shouted Sarah Jane. 'Female or not, I'm as good as an ignorant native, I hope!'

'I never said good!' he shouted back. 'Good is nothing! It's man's business, can't you see that?'

She could not, and he could not explain. He went on rubbing himself with fat, and Sarah Jane stared at the fire.

'S'Jane,' muttered the boy after a time. She turned her head stiffly and stared at him. 'Will you lend me your comb?'

Outraged, Sarah Jane ripped the possum-fur string over her head, threw the comb at him and retreated into her bark shelter. When she woke in the dawn he was gone.

2

Alone, Sarah Jane felt like a tiny beetle in the hand of a giant. 'You are Sarah Jane Tranter,' she reminded herself.

The only person in the world, her woeful mind replied.

'Fiddle-faddle!' snapped Sarah Jane. 'A person can't walk without falling over settlers and bushrangers and such! I could go after that dratted boy if I'd a mind.' But she knew she would not; and without him there was nowhere to go.

His fire still smouldered. Her comb was hung on a stick, with the boy's knife, now worn very thin, tied to its string for her to use. Sarah Jane made hideous faces at it. She would go to the sea, and the boy might find her if he chose.

She left the knife in her shelter with her possum furs and comb, lit a firestick, and set off down the slope. There was a little stream to travel with, and the voice of the sea, and nuts and fruits and nectar to gather. At dusk she made her fire to bake roots and keep the night safe. At daylight she saw, beyond the scrub, a heath-covered wall of dunes.

The boy had left when the stars told him morning was near. He went fast, looking for what he had seen from above: the sea, the hills of rock that rose out of it, the dunes marching towards them. It was not far. Soon the journey might be over and he was still alive. He was already far west along the beach — taking his gift of fire to Loo-Errn, uninvited and without the law. He had not told S'Jane that that meant death.

Now he could see the magic country of Marr-na-beek, and the hills of Wamoom springing out of the sea, but not yet the islands and mudflats of which his grandfather told. It was evening and he was hungry, but he would not venture to take food from Loo-Errn. Feeling with his feet in sand and mud, he took pippis and cockles from the sea.

In the heath he ate them raw, to show no fire. Then he lay and watched the stars and listened to the sea, wondering if he would hear it tomorrow night; and at last he fell asleep.

It was easy to wake when night turned towards morning. The heath and the sea lay under mist, white in the starlight with the dark hills of Wamoom rising out of it. The boy found dry sticks and carried them with him, walking along the edge of the sea in and out of the mist.

In his stomach fear lay quietly asleep. He had lived with it through a long time of thinking and planning; now danger was too close. He was coming where strangers might not come, trusting his little magic and the old reverence of fire. If his thinking was wrong it was too late for fear.

The stars grew pale and a finger of wind stirred the mist. The boy could see low shapes of islands lying between himself and Wamoom, and the mist curling among those mystic hills. It was time: he carried his sticks to a dry place and laid them together and made fire.

He stood over it singing as he had learnt, and the fire leapt and the boy's scar began to glow. He raised his arms and sang, and sprang upward on the flames; away on the magic hills the mist gathered and swirled. It rose into the sky, clothing a mighty figure that looked down with dark, mysterious eyes. A long arm swathed in mist reached over the sea. Loo-Errn called him to come.

Sarah Jane climbed the dunes to look down at the wrinkled sea, and ran down to the beach. The little waves tugged at her ankles and dragged the sand from under her feet. The big ones tumbled her in seaweed and rolled her ashore. The water was cold from the ice far down the world, yet the shock of it warmed her.

She roamed along the beach in sea and sun until she was hungry, and went back to the dunes to find salt-tasting pigface and portulaca. When she lifted her eyes, a stranger was coming near along the dunes. Sarah Jane sprang up to run, but the woman called out as if she were a friend.

'Ah. There you are.'

She was an odd figure: short, narrow at the shoulders and wide at the waist, with almost no neck. She walked in a sliding way, arms hanging loose and hands turned out, fingers fluttering. She had pale round eyes in a smiling face, pale sleek hair and a sleek white gown. She looked absurd, yet hauntingly familiar.

'Enjoying yourself, are you?' said the woman, falling easily down and sitting with her feet together. She fluttered her fingers on the sand. 'Sit here, do, and stop gaping. We were bound to meet again one time or another.'

Sarah Jane dropped down. She had seen that the woman was like a great white fish, and her fluttering fingers like fins; and that each, even the thumbs, wore a broad silver ring. Except the right index finger, which was bare. 'Are you —? Was it —?' Not finding the words, Sarah Jane held out her own hand with its silver ring.

The woman smiled and preened a little. 'Don't trouble with thanks. It was a small reward for saving me, and thanks enough to find you happy, as I see you are.'

Sarah Jane supposed she was, for a fish

woman who could change her shape would very likely know. She stammered, 'Will I grow up some day, then, ma'am!'

The Fish Woman laughed. 'No, child, never fear. Growing up leads to death, and that's a poor reward. No, I've given you the freedom of water, and it's yours until you give it back.'

'I can't give it back, ma'am. The ring won't come off.'

'Silly child! When you *choose* to give it back the ring will *fall* off.'

'And then will I grow up and go back to my people?'

The Fish Woman frowned a little. 'You'll become whatever is natural and go wherever is right.'

Sarah Jane thought about that. 'If it was to be natural,' she said carefully, 'I think I might be quite old by this.'

'That's possible. Would you wish it?'

'I don't know, ma'am. Only — I might wish not to be lonely and wild. I might wish to be back in a house with a kitchen, and people telling the goings-on. I've done nothing but run off with the salt mutton and the clothes on my back! I never did break the gravy boat, it was Cook did that!'

'You would wish to become an old woman in a kitchen?'

The round eyes rolled at her, and Sarah Jane wilted. 'No, ma'am,' she whispered. 'Only I don't like to be a devil.'

'I don't see the harm. You look hearty enough. Perhaps you don't know your gift.'

'Oh yes, ma'am! I never could swim before and now I've such a feeling for water and rivers, I seem to know them.'

The Fish Woman waved her white hands. 'But have you ridden them underground where stone sparkles like frost? You could do that. Have you rolled with the clouds and flashed with the lightning in a storm? You could do that. And the sea, what do you know of the sea?

'I love the sea! My father always spoke of it.'

'Did he tell of the deeps where the fish are

lit up with lights? Or the drowned cities where dolphins ring the bells? Or the gardens and forests of the sea swaying in the tides?'

Sarah Jane shook her head. She was entranced.

The Fish Woman leaned close and whispered. 'Can you guess why I'm here? It's to visit the ancient sea where I was made. And can you guess where it is? Hidden under the land! But it will come back. Water is never lost.' She somehow rose to her feet. 'No, child, you must not return your gift until you know it. Come; you must visit the sea's gardens, and its waterfall, and the beach where there are gems instead of shells. She turned away through the dunes and down to the sea.

'You know so much, ma'am,' said Sarah Jane, following, 'do you know the boy? Him with the gift of fire?'

The Fish Woman said, 'Ah.'

'He's not grown more than me. Will that be till he gives back fire, do you suppose?'

'Very like,' said the Fish Woman.

Sarah Jane was comforted, for she could not think that the boy would ever give back fire. She went with the Fish Woman into the sea, feeling so excited that it was like being afraid.

Waves dragged her under and whirled her like a leaf. She went under them with the Fish Woman and saw the bright surface above, and the swirling sand below, and shining bubbles and swimming fish, and fields of seagrass swaying. The seals came, sleek and flowing — she could touch a flipper or a tail — she could swim and turn like a seal, snatch air and dive down like a seal! If this was being a devil, it was more than she had thought.

There was a great forest of kelp as tall as trees, its stems going down into darkness, its long green ribbons swaying under the glassy roof of the sea. Fish lived among them like birds; and Sarah Jane darted with the fish, she was a bird in the forests of the sea. Deeper down, in great granite rocks, she and the Fish Woman glowed with a green-white light among the sponges and corals and starfish, anemones and sea-urchins.

They ate seaweeds and sea-fruits and oysters. At night they rested on the sea, and slept while the tide carried them to and fro.

By day they swam into great caves where underground rivers poured into the sea. They followed the caves far under the land, into water that was soft and sweet, and saw crayfish and eels and the bones of giant animals dead long ago. Beams of light struck down like swords, and they looked up through clear water to blue sky and pine trees far above. Tall, silken tresses of weed moved with the water. Green gardens bloomed, swaying together like dancers, every stem and leaf precise. And Sarah Jane knew she had seen all this before, in the dreams of the Sleeping Pool.

They went back to the sea and rode on storms and saw ships lying wrecked and buried in the sand. The sea was full of wonders, and the Fish Woman knew the stories of all the ship-wrecks. The upper water was sunlit green and gold by day, and at night the stars glinted on it.

The boy woke at dawn on the beach, not knowing how he came there. In his mind he carried the words of Loo-Errn, and the memory of dark, knowing eyes; and for a long time he lay still, holding the memory, not noticing the beach. When at last he stood up, he saw the old and broken wreck of a ship in the bay. He had not seen it there before.

He was suddenly anxious to find S'Jane and hurried back along the beach. He could not find the place where he had eaten and slept; the heath was too old, or it was torn by winds. Only the edge of the land was the same; he found his way by that and the view of Wamoom.

He slept by the little stream he remembered, and next morning climbed to the camp above. It had been empty for a long time. Fragments of charcoal under the weeds showed that S'Jane had not buried the fires. Sheets of bark lay rotting where the shelters had been. There was a bulge under the bark that had been S'Jane's: he tore at it in terror, but there were no bones under it. There were only her possum-skins stiffened and rotting, and the horn comb and the knife.

He took up the comb and knife, trying to think what to do. Worry mixed with terror and turned it into anger. He had *told* her he had to go alone to Loo-Errn: why couldn't she wait in the proper way, and where was she now? He raged and shouted and threw stones and stamped on the possum-skins.

Sarah Jane and the Fish Woman turned south over meadows of seagrass and found a current running east. They saw dolphins playing, and devilfish, and a great whale with small, sleepy eyes. The current hurried them on.

'How far?' asked Sarah Jane, suddenly anxious; for days and nights had slipped by and the boy might be waiting. He might go on alone, and she could not fancy being a devil without him.

'Far enough,' said the Fish Woman, looking

at the stars. 'Take a very deep breath, now, and hold my hand.'

The current closed round them like a squeezing hand and rushed them down into the deeps: faster and faster, down and down and down. Sarah Jane clung to the Fish Woman's silver rings. It was like whirling and tumbling in the middle of the world. It was the waterfall under the sea.

They came into dark, quiet water where strange creatures were lit with blue-green light and drifted by like comets. There were small, bony fish with huge mouths, and creatures with long, frail arms, and others with lacy, wavering shapes. The Fish Woman would not stay, but rose quickly through the quiet water to the stars.

'Would it be the tide makes the waterfall, ma'am?'

'No, child, it's the winter coming, turning the current around. There's no fall in summer.'

In sunlight they found an island, with a rocky bay under looming hills. Far north, where the sea met the sky, lay a smoky haze that the Fish Woman said was the mainland. Sarah Jane found honey and seeds in the scrub. She did not like to help herself to shellfish in case of some mistake, for hadn't she once nearly eaten the Fish Woman? She drank fresh water dug from the sand, and rested on the beach.

But the island felt strange and uneasy. The sun was too pale and blue, the air too hazy; and somewhere, surely, was a wailing cry that Sarah Jane could not catch. She drifted into sleep and heard voices mourning, and woke and could not hear them. And the sun was bluer, and the air smelled of smoke. She was uneasy.

'Here, child!' said the Fish Woman, coming from among the rocks. She tipped something into Sarah Jane's hand.

'Pebbles,' said Sarah Jane. There were three, like bits of frosted glass with a sparkle here and there.

The Fish Woman laughed kindly. 'Gems, my dear.'

'I declare! They're dull for gems.'

'No more than most. Polishing makes them bright.'

'And if I was to polish them, ma'am, I've still no way to carry them. I'd lose them for certain.' She faltered, seeing the Fish Woman displeased. 'You're so kind — but I must go back. I think the boy must be angry. I was to wait, you see.'

'Then it's he must wait.'

'He'll not do that. He'll go about burning the country. And indeed there's a great fire somewhere, making all this smoke.'

'That's far off on the mainland. You're safe here.'

'Ma'am, I could never stay in this sad place. People have been lost or mourning here, I almost hear them. I must go back and find the boy.'

'Then you must make your own way,' said the Fish Woman tartly.

Sarah Jane lifted her chin. 'I've my ring, not fallen off. I thank you for it, and for showing me the sea and the gems.' She bobbed in farewell, and waded into the ocean.

It was bad to be alone with only a silver ring. The eastward current caught Sarah Jane, and she thought she could feel the waterfall dragging her down. 'I'll not go, then!' she cried. 'I've a ring, I'll thank you to mind!'

That brought the dolphins: dark shadows gliding, white undersides gleaming. They opened their beaklike snouts to grin, and their eyes twinkled under domed brows. They circled and slid, inviting Sarah Jane to come. When she surfaced for air, a dolphin was snorting beside her. When she dived, they met her with twitters and grins. There was no fear left.

She went with them under the glassy roof of the sea. Night came, and she dozed on the surface while a blunt head nudged her or a broad back lifted her. Jellyfish drifted by, sketched in their own pale light. She heard the underwater twitter of dolphins, and their trails were lit in streaks and swirls of comet-light.

The sea rose in a great, slow swell and poured them all towards land: Sarah Jane and the jellyfish and the dolphins.

Once she woke with a start. Smoke dimmed the stars, and through it came a long finger of light, sweeping over the sea, probing and searching. It came again; and again. Sarah Jane tingled with fear, until at last she remembered her father's tales and cried, 'It's for the ships! It's a lighthouse!'

Next she was awakened by a strange, throbbing sound that troubled her. The dolphins had gone: perhaps land was near, or a school of fish. The darkness ahead was jewelled with fires, but morning soon dimmed them and showed her the ship. It lay south of her, travelling east, throbbing as it went and sending up a tall column of smoke. At first she thought it was on fire; then she saw the chimney between its masts, and a great wheel at the stern chopping up the sea.

Sarah Jane felt lost and shaken, as she had on the day when she knew the king was dead.

Ships had changed; she did not know them now. The land loomed massive and forbidding through the smoke. She knew she could never find the boy.

3

At daylight the boy stood high on the cliffs to watch for S'Jane. He thought she must surely have gone to the sea, and perhaps she might come back.

At first he had been too angry to think. In his burning rage he had loosed the fire and watched it leap through the land, hoping S'Jane would come running with the lizards and wallabies and bandicoots. She did not, and he rode the fire over trees, and the Magooya flew with him on giant wings; it was an eagle with red, fierce eyes. He saw animals die and houses burn and men fight for them, and his grandfather's face dark and angry in the smoke.

When he had seen all that, he lay in a cave for two days without food; and at last he remembered the sea.

He did not look for S'Jane amid its humps and hollows; they were too hazy with smoke. He saw the beam of light sweep by and knew it was white men's magic. In the smoke, he did not see the ship at all. He only watched the hazy beach and the ruffled edge of the waves, looking for something that moved; and at last he saw S'Jane.

The sea, foaming in between rocks, brought her ashore and left her. It had carried her for so long that she felt too heavy to move, and could only crawl up the sand. She was weary from ships and wind and gulls and dolphins, secret gardens and waterfalls, and the smashing of sea on rocks. She did not see the Magooya till it hung over her and screamed, its red eyes glinting, its legs like the branches of trees and its talons like meat-hooks.

Sarah Jane sprang up. 'Get off, you nasty brute!' she shouted. 'Anno Domini!

Catastrophe! Pickle-barrel!' She made hideous faces at the eagle, lolling her head and tongue in a dreadful imitation of someone hanged. From habit she shouted to the boy for help — and like magic he came running and shouting from the cliff. It was such a relief that Sarah Jane had to hide her face on her knees, while the Magooya swung away on its enormous wings.

She looked up when she saw the boy's feet standing near. He was frowning down, with her comb hung on its string round his neck. 'Did you find your knife!' asked Sarah Jane.

He would not answer, for the knife was in his belt plain to see and he was remembering to be angry.

'Your fire smoked all across the sea,' said Sarah Jane, 'I told her it was you; she that gave me the ring. She's a woman more than a fish, and rings like mine on every finger but one. I said you were burning the country, but she'd not bring me back though it was she took me off. I came alone all the way, but for the dolphins. Is the food burnt! Shall I bring fish?'

He could not scold or blame her for a fish woman with silver rings, but neither could he forgive her at once. He frowned and muttered, 'You can't climb with fish.'

They climbed to a ledge, wriggled up within a cleft, and reached a forested plain with mountains beyond. Smoke hung among the branches, but the forest had not burnt.

'I never!' cried Sarah Jane. 'I thought every stick was gone! I took it for a right-down rampaging fire!'

'It was!' said the boy proudly, throwing up his head. 'It rampaged in the hills from Marr-na-beek to here. Your people ran about like ants, putting it out.'

'And you riding the fire, I don't doubt, and spoiling all the country. Why has it stopped?'

'Night put it out; and the sea, might be. I let it go.'

'Thank you kindly. And you've burnt all the food?'

'Have sense, S'Jane. There's lizard and

bandicoot and roots cooked and still hot. There's this place and others not burnt at all; and the streams and the sea.'

'A stream, then, for I'm starved for food and sweet water, and sticky with the sea. Soon I'll tell you of the dolphins, and the water-forests, and a ship that pushes itself along.'

They went through an ugly, blackened forest where trickles of smoke still rose from trunks and fallen bark. Careful not to burn feet or fingers, they gathered the baked tubers of daisies and grass-orchids, the cooked shoots of grass-trees and palms, and roasted caterpillars and moths. When the sun went down they reached a stream in cool, moist scrub between two hills. The fire had leapt right over it.

The boy wove shelters of branches and made a fire. Sarah Jane washed in the stream, and sat in its water unbraiding her hair. It was still damp from the sea, and as she loosed it the comet-light out of the sea flared through it. 'Where are we going now?' she called. 'What do you have in your mind?'

He would have answered shortly, still punishing her for his worry and fright, but he was humbled by the flash of green-gold light in her hair. He said, 'West and north to the dry lands, and the lake where the water walks about. To find my Great Ancestor, all in shining stone, from the time when the land was made. I have to give him my grandfather's axe.'

When the words had finished running through her head she said, 'You saw Loo-Errn, then.'

He nodded. Later he spoke softly in the dark and told her more: of Wamoom springing out of the sea, and of walking towards it with his life in his hands; of the mist and the tall, white figure that it clothed, and how he had called to it with fire and Loo-Errn had answered. He spoke of power and wisdom, but not of any secret lore that he was given or any words that were said. Sarah Jane too was humbled and asked no questions.

When they were asleep the Magooya came

softly to their fires: not as a giant eagle but tiny, in its own shape. It watched there all night, for in all this changing land only the boy and girl were still the same.

The Great Ancestor

1

*W*here are the dry lands, and the lake where the water walks about?'

'North across the land to the Big River, then west till it comes to the sea. North in the hills to the dry lands, and west to the lake.'

'Back across the land to the Big River? Why must we go that long, hard way? There's the coast going north as I saw from the sea; it must come to the river at last, and fish and oysters to eat all the way.'

'Oh, S'Jane! I have to do what Loo-Errn said. There might be other rivers, and how will I know?'

'I can tell you, I should hope.'

But the boy would only say, 'On the coast there are too many people and I don't know the countries.'

'Fiddle-faddle,' said Sarah Jane. 'The river will come to the coast for all of that.' But she would not fight with him again.

They climbed rugged, burnt slopes, and looked down at a bay crowded with masts and spars and chimneys. The boy had seen it while he rode the fire.

'It's those ships you said. They come in and never go out; might be they can only push one way.'

'What a fandangle! They push all ways to get here. But so many! It's like one of those battles.'

'There's a town up the bay; and roads and mobs of people.'

'That's lively. We might come back when you've done with this Ancestor. Here they'll not know of Mistress Allen or devil's eyes. They'll not hurt us.'

He said, 'Might be. What do they do to children that don't grow up?'

Sarah Jane had no answer.

On the high plains the forest had been thinned or cleared. There were sheep and cattle and barking dogs; and Sarah Jane stared at a

123

farmhouse built of sawn timber, with glass windows and a shingled roof although it was so far from Sydney Town. It had flower gardens all around.

'Come on, S'Jane, it's just a house.'

She turned on him. 'It's grand enough for town. I don't doubt there's a cook and a kitchenmaid. But I daresay to a little native boy it's the same as a hut.'

The boy was troubled. 'Do you want to go back to your people?'

She made her devil's face. 'A higgle-piggle female in a paperbark skirt? "Please, ma'am, do you want a scullery-maid? I'm Sarah Jane Tranter, near twelve years old, that ran off from Mistress Allen thirty years ago with the food from her kitchen." What a to-do it would be!'

They went on towards northern hills and the Big River. Tracks criss-crossed their way, and once a wider trail. The boy said, 'It's a road to that town.'

Sarah Jane pounced on a yellowed news-sheet caught in a shrub. 'The news of England! Some gentleman has dropped it, bringing it from town as Captain Allen would!' She smoothed it carefully.

The boy scoffed. 'What good is it? You can't read it!'

Sarah Jane turned pink under her brown. 'I might. Some of it.' She bent over the sheet. At first the print looked only mysterious; then letters began to emerge, and she struggled to remember the teaching of the Reverend Jenkins. All she could read was a date, and she read it bleakly. 'Eighteen fifty four … near sixty years. A person's life.' The boy was silent, and she folded the paper and tucked it into her possum-skins.

At evening by the fire she brooded over it again. There was a drawing: a track crowded with wagons and people. The artist had put in a grass-tree and a wallaby near the track. Sarah Jane was puzzled. She went over and over the words under the drawing.

'Gold,' she muttered at last, and hunted for

more words. In a while she showed the drawing to the boy. 'Look: people going to dig for gold. It's called a gold rush.'

'What's gold, then?'

'I should hope anyone knows that. It's what sovereigns are made of, and rings, and the Reverend Jenkins's watch. Gold's treasure.' She frowned at the paper. 'One of these grass-trees, look, and a wallaby. And over here, a picture drawn of a grand new building; and see all these fine goods, worth a fortune: just landed from a ship, the merchants say.'

He said, 'I showed you the ships.'

'Fiddle-faddle to the ships. Don't you see this is not the news of England? It's the colony's own news, printed special. The gold is here, and hundreds of people coming to find it. They say the ships can't sail for the way the sailors run off after gold. What should we do, two naked devil-children in this fandangle? It's all towns, and fine shops, and gold, and grand houses in the forest. Where should we go?'

'West and north,' said the boy, 'to the dry

lands and the lake where the water walks about.'

'And there we'll find a new town and your Ancestor dug up for gold, and everyone staring at us for naked savages.'

'You know nothing, S'Jane. A Great Ancestor is more than gold, and people won't stare if we creep by at night.'

Sarah Jane gave the newspaper to the fire. Everything was changed, and she and the boy were left behind. They were like ants unseen in the grass, following their own secret paths.

The days went by and still they went north, seeking the Big River. Trees and streams dwindled; they climbed stony rises in a lonely country. Little spirits came out of the rocks at night: they were like small Hairy-Men with claws. Sarah Jane gave up combing her hair because of the way they stared, and the boy refused to look at them at all. The journey went on; and one day, from behind a screen of bracken, the children gazed at a road.

Yellow dust hung over it, and over the

people who trudged on it. They carried tools and blankets and pots and bundles. A dusty dray was drawn by a dusty horse. Bullocks pulled a wagon loaded so high that it swayed. Women carried children; people rested under trees; a coach rocked by, guarded by horsemen with guns. It was like the picture in the newspaper.

The boy tugged at the girl. They crept away. 'Gold rush indeed!' gasped Sarah Jane. 'There's not gold enough in the world for all of those!' They lay hidden till dark, cooking lizards on a tiny fire among rocks. By then the hubbub had died; there were only scattered camps and fires, and voices speaking or singing. The children crawled like puppies over the road, dived into scrub and fell into a gully.

'They'll have heard us, surely!'

'If they have, we're only wallabies.'

'I wish I might see them at work, digging the gold.'

'That wild mob? Have sense, S'Jane.'

'They're wild in their trouble to find it;

they'd be happy then, and kind. Don't you care to see your people happy, now they run away without spearing?'

'I care for my grandfather,' said the boy distantly, for he had never known the others. He added, 'They run away now I'm a devil. When I was real they ran *after* me.'

They slept to the sound of distant singing; and the hills stood over them, a long, dark shape against the sky.

By day those hills seemed to draw back as the children went towards them; but it was easy walking, in open country without roads or noisy crowds. They aimed for a ridge that the boy had chosen because it ran easily up the hills, and because a stream ran out from below it. In time they met the stream and followed it, though Sarah Jane complained that it was muddy. 'What's troubled it? In a dry time there's no call for dirty water.'

'Sheep, might be,' said the boy, remembering the overlanders' trail; and a rough track did follow the stream.

It was lost at last, in a dark, wooded gully, and the ridge itself loomed over them. It was sunset; the boy had killed an echidna and carried it dangling from a stick. They climbed the ridge to camp and make a fire — and from that height they saw that there were already fires far up the gully. Strong white columns of smoke rose over the trees, and new ones began to climb while the children watched.

'We must find another ridge,' said Sarah Jane.

The boy frowned, for this one led to the hilltops. 'Not till we've seen what's there,' he growled.

'A nasty lot of bushrangers, I'll be bound.'

'Bushrangers would have one fire. We should go and look.'

'You do as you choose,' said Sarah Jane. 'I'll not go near.' But after all she could not wait alone, and crept after him in the dusk. They followed the ridge upward as far as the smoke, then stole down its side from tree to tree. The boy pointed, and they crouched among bushes to look.

The fires were down in the gully, each fire outside a tent. A small village of tents was spread among the trees. People stirred pots and pans on the fires, and the smell of cooking rose with the smell of smoke. Between the tents ran the stream, a thread of water in a wide, shallow bed that the rains would fill. Now the bed was torn into holes and heaps of gravel, littered with tubs and buckets and strangely shaped boxes and shovels and picks. Water trickled among them, listless with mud.

Sarah Jane made a word with her lips: 'Gold!' The boy nodded and tugged at her to come away, but she crossed her eyes and poked out her tongue, so he waited. These were her people of Lord Eighteen Fifty-four, come from over the sea in ships. She gazed at them, tense with eagerness, and the boy looked too.

They were tired men, resting and eating. Their faces were bearded, and they mostly wore red or blue shirts. Their tents were fine and new, old and shabby, or a blanket thrown over a branch. Nearest was a bark hut where a woman in a shawl made tea; washing hung on a rope outside, and some of the garments showed that there were children in the hut.

Suddenly the boy was jolted upright: Sarah Jane had sprung up and was running down the slope from tree to tree. Had she gone crazy? He could only watch. She reached the line of washing: it waved and swung. She was running back, carrying something. The boy gritted his teeth, and then the trouble began.

Someone saw the swinging line of clothes; someone saw a running shape. Someone shouted 'Thief!' and the shout ran from tent to tent: 'Thief! Thief!' Men with firewood and picks and guns came running, for thieves were the evil of the goldfields. The boy shouted, 'S'Jane!'

She came scrambling up the slope, clutching some dark stuff. He snatched it, threw it down the hill and seized her hair. 'Run!' he ordered, for a roaring pack was near.

The men shouted and waved their weapons; their beards bristled and their eyes glared. The boy looked for somewhere to hide, and a great, fiery dog sprang in front of him. The Magooya had come. The boy tugged and shouted again: 'Run!'

And Sarah Jane ran. The men were terrifying, and she had not thought to steal; only to be respectable and not a devil-child. She ran with the boy to their camp, and took what he gave her to carry, and followed him down the far side of the ridge into a shelter of rocks. There she sat down and sobbed.

'What's the good of that?' barked the boy.

Sarah Jane wept on.

'But for the Magooya we'd be dead or locked up.'

Sarah Jane laid her head on her knees and sobbed.

The boy sighed. 'A devil got into you. What did you steal?'

Sarah Jane sniffed and raised a defiant face. 'You should know, since you threw it away.'

'Some useless gown to tear and rot?'

Sarah Jane rose with dignity and went away.

The boy made a fire, cooked the echidna, ate his half and lay thinking. Some time later, Sarah Jane came back. She found her share of the echidna and laid it on the fire to clear the ants. In the darkness the boy spoke.

'It's right, what you said. This way's too hard, with the people and roads and gold. We'll go west and find the sea, and the Big River running out.'

'I'm sorry for the gown,' muttered Sarah Jane, for she could not fight with the boy. They must keep together.

In the morning they turned west. For a long time they walked: first along the hills, and then over ridges that spread like fingers, with valleys and little streams between. Sometimes they had to avoid a cluster of miners' tents, and once or twice a low-roofed house alone in the empty country.

They found high, rolling plains where ancient rocks stood frowning and the west wind sang like the sea. Sarah Jane spun fur into string for a belt, and made a new skin bag to hang from it. Often a fire-lizard came to their fire; and once, with warning cracks, a great white owl swooped over.

'Tarradiddle! Parramatta!' cried Sarah Jane. The owl turned into a dingo rolling its red eyes and snapping with its teeth. 'Go away!' she called, and the dingo became an old man, tall and wispy with huge, red eyes. Sarah Jane sighed. 'What's to do, then? What does the creature want?'

'To frighten us, might be,' the boy suggested.

'I hope we'd not fear a thing that saved us from all kinds of wild men. It's only a pity it's got so set in its ways.' She put her thumbs to her ears, waggled her fingers and lolled her tongue. The Magooya went away, cracking with anger and weaving among the branches.

They travelled for a long time: while new settlers came to the lonely western countries, and towns were built, and flocks and herds driven over plains as wide as the world. They travelled while explorers rode away on camels to search for vanished seas and found only red, rolling sands and empty rivers. There were hot days and cold nights, when the stars hung bigger and brighter because they hung so low. There were wet times when gullies were suddenly streams, and dry times when Sarah Jane found secret water hidden under rocks. Time grew so long that they almost forgot where they were going; but at last, one day among marshes and ridges, they stumbled on a track.

'Where did it come from, then, so sudden?' Sarah Jane demanded; for the track wound on through the wide, low country, going east and west with no end or object in view.

'Some gold-digging place, might be,' said the boy.

They followed the track, nervously at first; stopping often to listen, keeping their own fires small and watching for the smoke of others. It seemed only a track lost in the bush and going nowhere, and at last they forgot to be careful. It was then that they heard the sound.

It grew out of silence, little by little: a strange, warbling music. It sounded unearthly to the children, and they quickly climbed into a tree. The sound came nearer and grew into a kind of chorus.

'Devils!' hissed the boy, preparing to jump down and run. But the singers of the chorus were too near.

They came out of the west in a long line, trotting like ponies one behind the other, singing their strange chant. They were like small people but all of them the same, and so strange that the children had no doubt they were devils. If they had faces, they were hidden under wide, shallow hats with pointed tops. Under the hats were blue jackets and loose, blue trousers, and long rods across the shoulders with bundles and baskets hung from both ends. They passed under the tree without seeming to see it. When they were gone, the children tumbled down and ran.

2

The devils' warbling faded in the east while the frightened children ran west. A low ridge loomed, and trees lined a waterway of broken stone: they plunged into it and found a dark hole between rocks. They crept in, and crouched and listened.

No singing devils came. But slowly, out of the darkness, a cave began to grow: broad and low and safe, like a protecting hand; reaching back under the ridge. There was a flutter of bats and a stillness of moths. The children crept into it among grey shapes of rocks, to the edge of the deepest dark. They crouched under its low roof while the sun went down and evening came.

'I don't know the harm of a few devils,' Sarah Jane ventured at last, 'when they're all around and ourselves devils too.' She stretched her aching legs. 'It's a fine, safe place for camping.'

'Stay here,' said the boy. 'I'll get wood.'

'There's water near, if I had a firestick.'

He nodded and crept outside. Sarah Jane tipped roots and a lizard from her bag and filled it with big, grey moths from the walls of the cave.

The boy brought wood and built their fire. Moths fluttered into it, little bats flitted and swung, and rocks glittered mysteriously in the firelight. The boy tried not to look.

'Don't mind it,' said Sarah Jane, full of delight. 'It's only water-gems. And now I've the firestick, I'll find water.'

She took a burning stick into the dark. While he waited the boy fed the fire, and laid roots in ashes, and set a stone to heat for roasting moths. The firestick glowed again, and Sarah Jane came back. She did not speak but stared with wide eyes.

'What's wrong!' said the boy. 'Is there water?'

She nodded.

'What else?'

Sarah Jane found her voice. 'I — do declare I've found him. Your Ancestor, all in shining stone.'

Firelight flared in the boy's eyes, but in a moment he shook his head. 'No, S'Jane. I told you. Loo-Errn said where, and it's not here.'

'Fiddle-faddle to Loo-Errn! There's this great man wrapped in stone, and no water to be had for him lying in the way.'

The boy frowned. 'Sit down, then. We'll wait for morning.'

Sarah Jane stamped her foot. 'That's never — so dark as it is down there! I tell you —'

'Tell me nothing! We can't sleep by a grave, and there's night and blue devils outside. My Ancestor would speak, and I'd hear with another ear.'

He took sticks deeper into the cave and lit another fire, singing to it. Sarah Jane sat down and began to roast the moths, for she saw that he was closing off the passage with fire.

All night the second fire burnt, and in the morning the children took firesticks from it and crept down a long slope that was slippery with water and broken rock. The firesticks lit up spears and waves and waterfalls of sparkling stone. They were water-magic to the boy, but S'Jane had the silver ring.

Then a fallen column blocked the way, glittering like the rest. It had the shape of a sleeping man, as a weathered rock might have; but when Sarah Jane held her firestick near, a dark and hollow face looked out through the glassy stone.

The boy backed away quickly and Sarah Jane followed. 'Is he your Ancestor?' she whispered.

He shook his head but did not speak till they were in the cave. 'He's a man. It's only the stone makes him big, but how did he get inside? It's magic. He's some old Clever Man. Come away.'

They scurried outside. Under the tumbled rocks there was water; they drank, and washed away the death in the cave.

That day they stumbled on the track again,

and turned farther north to be free of it because the boy said it was a devil track. But sometimes in their westward journey they came on it again, and saw men riding horses, or people carrying loads and pushing hand-carts, or a flock of sheep travelling west in a cloud of dust. So they knew the settlements and goldfields of the east had reached out to these far western lands; the track was for men and not devils, and they could venture near.

They were resting beside it in a clump of mallee one day when a line of blue devils did trot into view. The shock kept the children still, frozen among the mallee trunks. Then, as the devils passed, Sarah Jane made a small, astonished sound.

'It's not devils! My father told me of them. It's Chinamen, see their pigtails!'

Looking up at their faces instead of down from a tree, even the boy saw that they were people. The Chinamen, smuggled ashore on a lonely coast and finding their own way to the goldfields, vanished east in the lonely land; and the boy and girl went west.

Ridge followed ridge, with water-washed silt and gravel lying between. Deep underneath them Sarah Jane felt the rushing of rivers, and water-gardens hidden under the land, and ancient bones in caves. She heard in her sleep the old, slow voice of the sea, telling of kelp forests where fish darted like birds; of lost ships, and storms, and bells ringing in drowned cities.

'The sea is near,' she told the boy; and at last, one day, they heard it roaring.

It lay beyond the dunes that the wind had piled into hills and carved into valleys. The children ran through the valleys and plodded up one of the hills. Below lay a beach up which the tide came sweeping, in great waves that rolled in from the ocean and smashed on the sand. The children slid down the sandhill and raced along the beach.

It ran north and curved west, far and far, until it melted into distance; and somewhere along its dazzle and haze the Big River must come to the sea. In the humps and hollows of the sandhills grew low scrub and tussocks of grass, torn and trampled by wind and storms; but between the humps there were sheltered hollows of warm, dry sand. Fresh water was buried there, sweet and cold. There were tracks of crabs and lizards and small, furry creatures, and dead scrub for a fire or a shelter, and straggling pigface with purple fruit, and sweet young shoots of grass.

It was a good coast to travel. The tide rolled up the long beach bringing fish; and when it ran out the wet sands bubbled where cockles and worms and little crabs were hiding. When the wind howled, the sand ran singing and stinging ahead of it. Far out near the sky there were ships with swelling sails, or with smoking chimneys and no sails.

For a long time the children walked, and the beach ran ahead and melted. The boy began to fear that the Big River was lost.

'Can't you tell, S'Jane? It's so big you ought to feel it. Isn't it near?'

'How can I feel the river when the sea's so strong? When it's near we'll find it, you'll see.'

But all they found was a strip of marshy sand behind the sandhills, as if the sea had been carried in by storms.

In time the swampy strip became a long, long lake running north and west in the shelter of the sandhills, cutting them off from land and melting with them into the distance. Its shallow water was crowded with birds: a good place to swim, or collect eggs and sedge roots. Sometimes a group of the brown people came there to gather food: a slender, quiet kind wearing the clothes of white people. The children would run off in the sandhills, or stay alone on the beach.

'Will they hunt us, do you suppose, so far away as we are? Or will they take us for devils and let us be?'

'Might be. Or might be they don't fear devils' eyes, now they have clothes.'

'Should we cross over to land and leave their country?'

The boy shook his head. 'It's quieter here. No tracks, or people after gold. If there's trouble we'll cross over.'

'Well then, you must take up the fire-lizard by your foot and let it ride on your belt. The poor thing's fandangled with all this water and sand.'

'If it's come all this way, why is it fandangled now? If it's a Magooya it can turn into a bird and fly.'

'You know it fears water. It needs help, such a little thing as it is. Gracious goodness, you were pleased enough to be the one helped.'

He did not believe that the fire-lizard and the Magooya were the same, but he could not be sure, and it was true that he owed the Magooya help for help. He gave her a smouldering look, scooped up the lizard and put it on his axe. The knife was now so worn and jagged that it was kept in Sarah Jane's bag for safety.

So the days went on, and the distant haze moved back, and at night long beams of light came out of it, probing across the sea for ships. Sometimes a beam probed into the dunes and woke the children in their nests of sand; and they knew that here, so far across the land, there were white people and new settlements.

A skyline of hills grew out of the distance; the lake opened wide among islands. Ships seemed to sail through the beach itself and pass into the lake; and at last they could see that the beach vanished into the sea. By then there were islands near, and the children could cross the lake from island to island with the fire-lizard in Sarah Jane's bag. 'It might be Big River water,' she told the boy while they rested on the shore. 'There's forests in it, and snow.'

He nodded. Long ago, beside the eastern sea, his grandfather had told him of the mighty lake far away at the mouth of the Big River. He remembered the stories of its making and its magic. It was not like the stories now.

There were ships churning up the water with great paddling wheels, purring through their chimneys like giant cats and towing long barges. There was a town cluttered with the masts and chimneys of ships. Men in short jackets and wide hats spoke in a way Sarah Jane called outlandish. Women hid inside their bonnets and wore skirts so wide that no one could come near. There were sheep and cattle and dogs and noise. It was so long since the children had seen or heard such things that they felt like strangers with nowhere to go; but Sarah Jane could not stop looking.

'How did it come here, so far as it is? We never saw.'

'We did. The river brought it; and ships, and that track.'

They skirted towns and farms, and hid from people. They climbed hills and looked down on more towns, with more sea beyond. At night the towns had flaring lamps on long poles to light the streets, and by day a fiery engine, puffing out smoke and hissing with steam, pulled a long line of coaches and drays faster than horses could gallop. Even Sarah

Jane was afraid.

The hills ran north, as Loo-Errn had said; and below them, to the west, a long arm of the sea reached into the land. Its coast was busy with settlers, but the hills were quiet. They held food and water, and sometimes a farm, and rocks and slopes to hide among. Once, in a gully, the children felt watching eyes and saw brown people among the trees, but they only looked and went away. They were slender like the others, and wore clothes.

It was slow work climbing among the hills. Sarah Jane gazed wistfully over a green valley to the sea. 'It's a long step to the dry country. I doubt we've taken the wrong way.'

The boy scowled because he was uneasy, and said rudely, 'You can't take the wrong way north.'

There came a night when they camped high in the hills, and in her sleep Sarah Jane heard a sound that wakened her. It was a high, sweet ringing, like one long note of music. In her sleep it was strong and strange, but awake she caught only faint echoes running into silence. She sat up under the stars to catch it, and saw that the boy sat listening too.

'What was it?' she whispered.

He put up a hand for silence. 'Listen.'

She listened. She could just hear it pulsing and fading, like the after-note of a bell. 'What *is* it?'

'My Ancestor, might be,' he muttered, not wanting to answer; for she was female, and white, and he believed she should not hear the sound at all.

'Do you hear him clear?'

'Clearer than before. Listen.' To him it was not an after-note but one endless, singing word like the never-ending word of the sea. He could not catch the word, but he thought it meant *time* or *forever*.

'Does he say where he is?'

The boy shook his head and said, 'Listen.' They listened till they fell asleep. In the morning Sarah Jane asked questions that the boy could not answer.

'Do you fancy he's near?'

'Nearer than before.'

'I wish he might speak.'

'He did. To me.'

'Tell me, then. What did he say?'

But the boy could not speak the Ancestor's word. He only growled. 'You're not meant to hear. It's a man's business.' Sarah Jane put her thumbs in her ears and wiggled her fingers.

Once, after that, they stood on a hilltop to watch the sun sink below hazy hills across the water; and the boy caught a moment of music, and Sarah Jane its echo. And once, at night, it sang among the stars where the smoke of ancient campfires shone.

At last, quite suddenly, the green country fell behind. There were no more towns or farms. The hills grew steep and gaunt and bare, wind-scoured and tilted and folded: hills left over from the making of the world. They drove the children down into scrubs of mulga, where there were no more glimpses of the sea.

All day they walked through the dry scrub

at the feet of the hills. They saw no one, though sometimes they found wheel-tracks, and there were trampled places where tall poles had been raised like the masts of ships. They carried a wire that drooped away towards the next pole, and Sarah Jane thought them ridiculous.

'Is it a Magooya-fence, do you suppose?'

'It's some work of your people,' said the boy darkly. 'Keep away, S'Jane.'

At night they went back between the hills, and camped where pools of water lay in the stream-beds. The hills loomed over them heavy with age, and stars rested on their peaks. Little Hairy-Men crept by, silent and afraid, going north to escape the white men. Shapeless spirits drifted like mist; owls watched, and mopokes called. Gazing at the fire, Sarah Jane felt the heaviness of time. She looked back through it, searching for her parents and their cottage in the east, but the pictures ran away down a long, long tunnel of years. 'I am Sarah Jane Tranter,' she told herself firmly, and looked at the fire-lizard instead.

'How long do lizards live?'

'Not long,' said the boy, staring at the fire. He too was looking down the tunnel of years. 'Magooyas do, might be.'

'My ring is loose. It turns on my finger.'

He said sharply, 'Keep your hand closed. Tomorrow I'll stick it on with gum.'

'It's safe enough, only that it wants the sea. Tomorrow we might go there.'

Next day they climbed a hill to look for the sea. West and north lay the end of the long inlet and the roofs of some small town. That kept them to the hills until the town was passed, and the sea gone, and the scrub was only grey-green bushes scattered over sandy, stony ground. The tall poles marched away, carrying their drooping wire across the empty land.

'Come back, S'Jane, it's not safe. The wire comes down and catches you, might be.'

The days went by. Clouds passed over; thunder rolled and lightning sprang.

Sometimes the northern hills were veiled in curtains of rain; sometimes the storm was near, and in the hills dry gullies became roaring torrents. Soon they were dry again, but the children would never camp in them.

There came a day when they climbed another hill and looked down on the dry lands. They lay bare under the setting sun, from the hills to the far, shining sky: yellow-brown, without green of grass or tree; speckled here and there with grey bushes, and strung across, from south to north, with that ridiculous wire sagging from pole to pole.

'Gracious goodness,' whispered Sarah Jane. 'It's only ants or lizards could go out there.'

'You can wait here,' said the boy.

'Fiddle-faddle. How will you find water?'

'It's not only ants and lizards go there. People do.'

'Not without they're born to it, poor souls.'

It was true, and the boy could not answer. He screwed up his eyes. 'There's a shine far out. Where the sun's going down, see. Water,

154

might be.'

Sarah Jane screwed up her own eyes. 'Sand, more like. Else it must be the sea, it goes so far.'

'Lake,' said the boy, suddenly certain. 'The lake where the water walks about.'

They gazed while the sun sank behind invisible hills. And from far away came a long note of music, pouring like the sea and ringing like a bell: the call of the Great Ancestor.

3

The Ancestor's call rang into silence and Sarah Jane sighed. 'It joins everything up,' she whispered. She was not sure what this meant, but it told the boy she had heard the music clearly.

They looked again at the dry lands while shadows crept across them to the west. Sarah Jane said, 'There has to be water if people go there. Born to it or not.'

'And shade. There are sort of cut-off hills, see? And sort of rivers. Some of these gullies from here must run out there.'

'Dry, for certain.'

'I know that, but we need shade. A river with banks would be best.'

'When they're all dry? A flat hill is shadier.'

'And then we run to the next hill? Have sense, S'Jane. A river has to *go* somewhere. Might be it goes right out to the lake, like a road. Might be there's water underneath.'

'Might be it goes a little way and there's only sand and stones.'

'Then you can come back, can't you?' he shouted. 'You *got* there by the river, so you know you can come *back* by it!'

Sarah Jane gave her sketch of a hanged man. It drove the boy downhill in a fury, leaving her to follow alone.

Three days later they found a stream that held water. It came into the hills from the east, under a tall peak whose lower slopes wore a forest of wide-spreading red gums. From there the stream ran north through a shady pool, and at last turned west into the dry lands. A straggle of red gum and casuarina went with it a little way. It was a wonderful, unexpected place to find, and the children leapt joyfully into the pool.

'There's been a storm,' said the boy. 'That one we saw. You can see where the water's run in.'

They camped by the stream for days. At morning and evening small wallabies came to drink, and emus and dingoes and little furry things. The forest was busy with birds. The boy ground his grandfather's axe to a new edge, and sharpened a digging-stick hardened in the fire, and shaped and balanced a new throwing-stick. Sarah Jane filled her skin bag with seeds and corms, and dug roots to hang in bundles from her belt. The fire–lizard appeared, watching with small, bright eyes as the children made ready for the dry lands.

'Tomorrow,' said the boy, 'we'll go a little way to see. We'll take everything with us, as if going was real, and see if we can carry it all.'

They left while night still hung between the hills, and followed the stream into the flat country. A few red gum and casuarina trees marked its way. By late morning there were only starved and stunted trees, and they could see none ahead. The stream had split into many channels where a little moisture lay; the sun poured out heat and the bare ground threw it back. Ahead, the strange poles pointed to the sky and their wire glinted.

'We can easily go back,' said the boy. But when they had rested they went on.

Waves of midday heat drove them into a patch of saltbush to crouch in small scatters of shade. While they waited they chewed leaves and seeds from the bushes, explored roots in search of woodgrubs, and dug a long tailed, grey lizard out of a burrow. Later, as they followed the stream west again, they dug another lizard from its hole in the bank.

'We should go back,' said the boy, looking back at the hills.

'There's no call,' Sarah Jane declared, 'with

the water still underneath.' She felt it beneath her feet.

'You should go back and wait. It's my business.'

'Man's business, I daresay.' She made her devil's face. 'I'll not go, then, when we've not crossed under the wire.'

The hills they had left became a rugged skyline stretching from south to north. The sun went behind one of the low, flat-topped hills that stood here and there in the dry lands. The mysterious wire came near, sagging over the channels of the stream and rising towards poles on either side. They rose tall and majestic over shrubs and pygmy trees, and near the top of each was some shiny thing to which the wire clung. The boy pointed to it with his chin.

'Watch out for that.'

Sarah Jane stared at the shiny thing, longing to know what it and the poles and the wire were for; and while she looked, the boy crossed under the wire. Nothing happened.

'Come on, S'Jane!'

She ran after him.

Now the wire swung behind them, cutting them off from the hills. 'We can still go back,' said the boy.

Instead they walked west in the cooling air until Sarah Jane felt limp, as if she had been a long time in the sea. 'There's some that gets hungry,' she grumbled. 'I don't fancy carrying bundles of roots for nothing.'

'It's not for nothing. It's in case.'

Sarah Jane crossed her eyes. 'Then I'll stop here and dig for water in case I turn into dust.'

The boy shrugged, laid his lizards on a stone, and went off to look for wood. It was hard to find in that flat, bare country, but at last he came back with sticks of dead saltbush to burn and a bundle of bluebush for shelter.

Sarah Jane had made a good hole and was sloshing wet mud with her stick. The boy reached down and let water settle into his hand. He tasted it and spat. Then he sat down with his head on his knees. Sarah Jane tasted the water. It was salt.

'I knew there ought to be trees,' growled the boy. He stood up wearily. 'Come on. We have to get back in the dark.'

Sarah Jane did not hear; she lay by the hole with her eyes closed and her hand reaching down. The sun had set and trickles of cool air flowed down the channels, but she did not feel them; she had fallen into a dream from long ago ...

Quietly and evenly like breathing, the water of the Sleeping Pool rose and fell. It washed her fingers gently, telling her many things, and slid softly away. It was cool and full of wisdom ... Cool water ... cool and still ... But now a thread of coldness curled through it, winding about her fingers and flowing into her palm. Cold water from dark caves, rising in search of the stars ... creeping higher, till her wrist was chilled and her fingers were aching with cold ...

The dream broke. Sarah Jane opened her eyes and spoke. 'It's all right. It's a night-well.'

'What sort of a thing is that?' asked the boy uneasily.

'There's no harm in it. It's good water that comes at night when people camp.' She cupped the cold water in her hand and began to drink. The boy watched keenly, and in a minute he was drinking too.

They cooked lizards and roots in the stream bed. Cold, crisp air came over the dry lands, and they huddled near the fire behind a shelter of bluebush. The fire-lizard buried itself in a bank, and they never saw it.

'Tomorrow we must walk longer,' said the boy.

In the night the cold grew chilling. Stars glittered and the air began to throb and hum. The humming grew until it filled the world and throbbed inside their heads. Sarah Jane curled herself into a tight, protesting ball. The boy lay rigid, whispering words to the fire, but no devils came near. The devils of the dry lands knew how the white man's wire sang in the cold. Some of them danced to it, some felt its throbbing in the poles, and some of them hid. The children lay as still as stone until that throbbing hum had died away, and when the night turned from black to grey they scurried away from the place.

'We'll go back,' said the boy doggedly.

'It must be some other way, then, for I've no strength to go near whatever it was. And thanks for nothing to your Ancestor; I daresay he's too grand to have us in mind.'

'You know nothing. We're not hurt, are we?'

The dry stream led them west. The sun threw the shadows of the hills after them and their own long shadows ahead. The dry land had shown them its cold and its heat; soon, when the ground baked and shimmered, it showed them its magical seas that could never be reached. They were seas of shining blue where waves danced and shimmered, seas that moved away as the children ran forward.

'Is it the lake?' cried Sarah Jane. 'The magic water that walks about?' For though she could see the water, she could not feel it.

'No,' growled the boy. 'That's real water.

This is devil water. The river's dry.' He kicked at the dust.

In the bad days that followed, the devil water often appeared and vanished. The children could never come near it. When they were hot and thirsty, they hated it because it was only a trick. When they were half awake, hungry and dazed by the sun, they thought it was real and stumbled after it.

They found no more night-wells in the stream's dry bed, but Sarah Jane's feet led them to the secret wells of the brown people, or to water cupped in rocks where the storm had passed. They learnt to walk by starlight and sleep under stunted mulga at midday, to trap moths at their fire and track lizards at dawn, to harvest saltbush seeds and chew the leaves of bluebush, and where to dig for roots. Sometimes, while they slept in the heat, the Magooya came on giant wings to make a shade. Sometimes it kept evil spirits away; and once, as the fire-lizard, it led them to a store of juicy snails under damp rocks.

The channels of the stream ran together and deepened; there were soft, damp places crusted over with white salt. And one day, quite suddenly, the stream bed ended; there was only a vast, flat surface of salt reaching away to the north and south and west. It had a bank, as a lake might have, and farther out there was blue water dancing in the sun. But the children knew that water.

'Must we go out there to find your Ancestor?'

'It's too hot now,' said the boy. 'There was bluebush back there. We'll go back and wait.'

For the salt lake seemed to cover the world, and on all its vast, dead surface there was nowhere to go.

4

When the children came down the stream bed again, the devil water had gone from the lake.

The westing sun lit the salt to dazzling gold. It ran away to the horizon, curving like the sea, and Sarah Jane turned her eyes away.

'Where did you have in mind to go?'

The boy had nowhere in mind. He took a quick, secret look and decided. 'Along the bank first, so we can find the way back.' He pressed his toes into the lake's crusty surface. 'It feels damp. Is there water underneath?'

'Yes, but it's no matter, for the salt. If we was to walk up there on the bank we might find good water somewhere.'

They mounted the bank. It was low and sandy near the stream but rose steeply as they walked; and soon they were high enough to see widely over the lake. It had a crinkled look, and there were dark patches as well as white. It was huge, and far across it, against the sky, the sun sank towards low, blue-hazed hills. Sarah Jane felt a stab of fear, and tossed her head to hide it.

'I should hope you know how to find your Ancestor.'

'It's too late now; we should find a camp and wait for dawn. There's swallows, see. There'll be water.'

They turned aside over broken, jumbled rock and found a tiny pool, deep between damp rocks that would soon be dry; the storm must have come here too. There were small, brown snails under the rocks, and Sarah Jane gathered handfuls while the boy explored the edges of the outcrop. He brought saltbush leaves, acacia pods rattling with seeds, some broken lengths of young tree-root, and a handful of wrinkled berries that had dried on the bush. Sarah Jane was astonished.

'How do you know they're good?' she cried.

The boy grinned. 'How do you know the snails are?'

'I should hope everyone knows snails. Do we know the berries and roots?'

'Of course; only the dry land makes them little, and we don't use them when there's something better.'

'Better? I can't think of something better.'

The snails took only a minute to cook but a long time to eat. They were good with salt-bush leaves. The ripe acacia seeds should have been made into cakes, but the children scorched them in the fire and crunched them like nuts while the tree-roots baked. When these had been pounded with rocks to soften them, a sweet, creamy sap could be chewed and sucked out of the fibres; and afterwards came the sun dried berries, like sultanas.

Sarah Jane stretched out beside the fire. The red gold of sunset had faded, and a young moon was brightening overhead. 'I've only one wish left,' said Sarah Jane, moon-gazing.

'It's bad to look at the moon. I've told you.'

She rolled over to please him. 'I wish your Ancestor might call to us.' The boy scowled at the fire. 'He did before, far away. Why won't he now we're near?'

The boy shrugged. 'How do I know?'

'You said you would, a long time ago in that cave. You said your Ancestor would speak to you, and you'd hear him with another ear. And he did; and we heard; and now we don't.'

'It wasn't him we heard, then.'

'It was you said so. I don't know what else it might be.'

'Some spirit that's not my Ancestor, and that's why you heard it too.' He would not say what he feared: that they had followed the wrong stream through the dry lands, and reached the wrong lake. The journey had been too hard; he could not say it might have been wasted.

But Sarah Jane said carefully, 'Some might call it a lake, only there's no water that walks about.'

Sheltered by rock and warmed by fire, they went unhappily to sleep.

A wind came sweeping over the lake. It found puddles of water left over from the storm, and swept them together and blew them across the salt. The young moon travelled down the western sky; and there came the deep, sweet voice of the Great

Ancestor. The children woke.

They did not speak to each other. As if they were still asleep, the boy took up his grandfather's axe and pushed its handle into his belt, and Sarah Jane followed him to the high bank of the lake. Below, moonlit water lay shivering in the wind: the water that had walked about. They hardly noticed it for the strong, sweet singing of the Ancestor. It drew them down the bank, through the shallow water, and over the salt-crust beyond.

There was a place where the bank had washed and crumbled, making a small cave scattered with fallen earth and stones. A ray of moonlight struck into it, and out of it welled the mighty, endless word of the Great Ancestor.

The children gazed and saw nothing; there was only a glimmer where something received the moonlight and gave it back. They looked and listened while the moon moved down the sky, and the cave floor darkened and the singing stopped. Then they crept in, and the boy laid his grandfather's axe in the cave and spoke the words that Loo-Errn had given him.

The glimmer returned though the moonlight had gone: some small thing shone milky blue and green in the face of a broken stone. There was a knotted cord, a kind of backbone, and fronds that had curled and curved in some ancient sea; and it shone because the ages, that had buried it in stone, had also turned it into opal.

The children did not touch it; they only crouched together in the cave. It was small and cramped, but it seemed to reach from the deepest sea to the tiniest, farthest star. The wind probed into it, but it felt warm and still and full of pity. The boy felt his grandfather's hand on his shoulder, the girl felt the love and care of home.

There were worlds of fire and shining fields of light, a vast darkness hung with stars, and wonders that could not be told. Earth grew, with its hills and rivers and birds and winds; giant beasts stomped over it, battles were fought in a flower bud and rivers flowed through a leaf. Kings and cities rose, and dark forests covered them over. There were voices crying, and music ringing, and at last a strong, deep silence that was full of peace and the making of life.

The children knelt there, dazed. At last they knew again that they were in the cave, and it was cramped and cold and dark; and the boy whispered, 'Come on.'

'Should we bury him again, in case?'

'No. He sings when the moonlight comes.'

They crept away through the shallow, wind-blown water. Back in their camp they did not try to speak of the Ancestor. Instead they fell suddenly asleep, tired out by the dry lands, and the worry, and at last the mystery and wonder.

The moon went down behind the far-off hills. A giant snake came slithering over the rocks. The fire-lizard saw it and became the Magooya: another mighty snake, cracking with anger.

By starlight, while the children slept, the two snakes fought, looping their great coils about each other and striking with their great heads. The Magooya fought bravely, but it was only a shape-changer; the other was Kuddi-Muckra, a giant man-eater of the salt lakes. He soon reduced the Magooya to its own fire-lizard shape, and swallowed it and hardly knew it. Then he slithered to the sleeping children and swallowed them too.

Now he set out across the dry lands, hurling his mighty body like a spear, for the Great Ancestor had called on him to make this journey. Twice he stopped to drink at starlit wells, and the water he drank lapped at the children inside him, and still they did not wake. He crossed under the wire that looped from pole to pole, and the spirits that haunted it fled and hid. 'Kuddi-Muckra!' they whispered in fear. 'Kuddi-Muckra!'

Before dawn the great snake reached the pool in the hills, and disgorged his meal and sped away. Through the heat of the day he lay coiled in a secret waterhole, and when night came he went slithering back to the lake.

The children woke sticky with slime, and jumped quickly into the pool. They were astonished to see it.

'It was a dream,' said the boy. 'We never went all that way and found the Ancestor. We're still here.'

'Fiddle-faddle,' said Sarah Jane. 'How could two have one dream? And what's become of your grandfather's axe and the digging stick?'

'Might be the Magooya brought us back,' said the boy; for in climbing out of the pool he had found the fire-lizard, lying sticky and limp. They washed it and laid it in the sun; and in a little while it staggered away to hide under dead leaves. The children trod carefully, anxious not to step on it, in case it had become the Magooya and carried them out of the dry lands.

They rested all day. The forest was cool and full of food, and when they felt warm they jumped into the pool. The boy found a sharp flake of stone to make a knife, and throwing and digging sticks to shape in the fire. He killed a bandicoot with one of them, and Sarah Jane caught catfish.

'I never thought to eat fish again,' she confessed, sitting by the fire that night while the stars rested on the hilltops. 'What with salt and dry seeds and no shade I thought we were done. I declare I'd have perished, only for having to find the next water.'

'You wouldn't. You liked the snails and stuff. And him.'

'Him ...' Sarah Jane's mind crept back into the cave. 'What was he telling us, do you suppose? And him so small, out of the old sea? There was so much, I was giddy.'

The boy's eyes darkened; he had never been able to grasp the Ancestor's word. He said stumbling, 'I think ... might be ... it was about forever.'

'So everything was in it,' said Sarah Jane slowly. 'All we know and all we don't. All that's happened and all that hasn't. I'd a right to be giddy, it's too much for one person. But I wish I might see it, so grand and fine as it is.'

'You have seen it. More than other people.'

'Me? I've no eyes for it. But I can tell you he's my Ancestor the same as yours; and we're people and not devils. Devils don't care. And look: here's the fire-lizard come.'

The boy moved his foot carefully to make room for the fire-lizard.

They rested for days, eating and growing strong. They made new tools and belts and bags, climbed trees and swam and shouted like children; yet they were troubled. Some cloud was hanging over them and they could not guess what it was.

Sarah Jane asked, 'Is your grandfather at rest, do you know?'

The boy frowned in surprise. 'Of course. You were there.'

'And it's all done as it should be?'

'There's nothing left.'

'Then I daresay we'll be going back.'

'Might be we can stay,' said the boy.

'What a tarradiddle, when you know we can never stay! We must always go on to another place for the food!'

'Might be we can stay a while. It's a good place, with the pool and food and no people.'

Sarah Jane felt a stab of something that hurt. She cried, 'And where will we go in the bad times, when the pool and the food are gone? The sea's far off, and people and towns all along it. There's only the dry lands near, and the hard hills. Do you fancy them in a bad time?'

The boy only stared sullenly, and they did not speak again until evening.

When they had eaten and were silent by the fire, the fire-lizard came to bask on a stone. 'We should take that back,' said Sarah Jane. 'It's only right.'

'We did, a long time ago, and it didn't stay.'

'You should think more of it, coming so far and helping. I do, being older. We've brought it out of its place; we should take it back to that Home of Fire.'

'Oh, S'Jane! You know it wants to come with us.'

'Come where?' cried Sarah Jane. 'We've nowhere to go and nothing to do! Before, there was your grandfather. Now there's only the fire-lizard. Without we take it back, we've nothing that wants doing. There must be *something*!' She jumped up and ran away into the dark.

The boy sat frowning at the fire. At last he arranged the sleeping-fires and lay in his shelter listening for Sarah Jane. She did not come. She was hidden on a branch above the pool.

Below, in the starlight, Hairy-Men were drinking. They knelt by the water with their wives and children, making soft, sucking noises. Two women murmured, a man grunted, and children stole glances into the tree. Soon they crept away, shadows melting into the forest to the north, and Sarah Jane suddenly wanted to cry.

When she stole back to camp the boy was

asleep, and she could not tell him there were people after all.

In the morning the boy woke first. The hills still laid their shadows on the edge of the dry lands, but he could not lie quiet; he was restless with the worry of the quarrel. He wandered into the forest, and climbed into the broad-spread branches of a red gum, and tried to see on the horizon the glitter of salt in the lake. Sounds reached him from below: a hollow, roaring noise and a man's shout. He climbed higher into the tree to look down.

There were three men. They rode the strangest beasts he had ever seen: long necked and long legged, with backs that rose into humps and with short, tasselled tails. The men sat behind the humps and just above the tails. A fourth beast carried a load and was led on a string; it propped with its long, ungainly legs and gave the hollow roar that the boy had heard.

He was not frightened. He could not have imagined beasts as strange as these, but he knew they were not spirit-beasts. They were ridden by white men who looked like soldiers, and white men had many strange beasts. He was only shaken to see them in the dry lands, riding their beasts along the poles and wire as he should have known they would. This place was not a safe retreat for blue-eyed children who never grew up; the pool must be an important watering place.

He watched the men out of sight, and climbed down and went back to the camp. Sarah Jane was sitting outside her shelter.

'There *are* people,' she told him at once.

'I know. I saw them. Where do you want to go?'

The question was too big and too sudden. Sarah Jane said, 'How should I know? You choose.'

'No, it's your turn. You came my way.'

Sarah Jane sat with her head on her knees, trying to sort out thoughts from feelings and to find the words. At last she said, 'I want to be real, not hiding away like devils.' She stole a look at the boy. He was frowning.

'Do you want to go back to your people?' he asked, for he remembered the farms, and the goldfield, and the stolen gown.

'Fiddle-faddle!' cried Sarah Jane, for she could not tell him how she longed for her people. 'I want to be in it! I want to do something that wants doing, and see things and know things! Like what people are up to now, and the year and the ships and the king!' She could never believe in the queen, for there had always been a king in the old days and she had heard of the queen only once.

'We know some of it. We know there's a lot of your people and we'll have to hide like devils.'

Sarah Jane tilted her chin. 'I daresay we might. There's sense in hiding when someone might see. But it's not decided; we'll stay if you choose.'

'We can't,' said the boy heavily. 'We have to take the fire-lizard back.' It was his way of giving in.

They spent most of the day in the forest, gathering gum and bulbs and roots to start them on their way. They swam and fished; and next day they turned south to find the Big River.

The Hairy-Men

1

They travelled south through the ancient, rugged hills; it was slow but safe. Sometimes, even here, they found wheel-tracks that they did not remember. 'Might be we forgot, or came another way,' said the boy.

'How long ago, do you suppose?'

'It makes no matter. Nothing's changed.'

Sometimes the fire-lizard came to their fire and sometimes they did not see it for days, but now even the boy knew it would guard them from spirits in the night. This, and the quiet of the hills, made them feel safe. It was a shock to be wakened one night by voices chattering near the shelters.

The children sat up in alarm. There were brown people: men and women and a few sleepy children, all wearing white people's clothes. Perhaps they knew the pool below the children's camp, and had walked through the night to reach it.

They chatted more loudly when the children sat up, but they did not seem angry. A woman seized Sarah Jane's digging stick, examined it and put it back; a man knelt to feel the boy's throwing stick and spoke in rumbling words.

'What did he say?' cried Sarah Jane, too frightened to hide it. The boy shook his head, for the man spoke a language he did not know. The man looked sharply and spoke again.

'Where from?' he asked, handing back the stick.

The boy answered sullenly, head down. 'Dry lands.'

'Where to? You talk, no hurt. Go where?'

'Big River,' muttered the boy, clutching his throwing stick.

'Keh,' said the man, thinking. 'Uncle belong you?'

'Grandfather,' said the boy, and made up his mind not to understand any more questions; he would only shake his head.

But the man did not ask any more questions. An old woman, grey haired and wrinkled, spoke a few words from behind, and he nodded and turned away. The brown people went farther along the hillside, chattering loudly, carrying sacks or herding children. They began to make fires and sleeping places, and to hand out food from the sacks.

'They've bread,' whispered Sarah Jane.

'Sh!' hissed the boy.

'They're taking off the clothes.'

'In case they catch fire in the night. When they're asleep we'll go.'

It was not to be so easy: the old woman came near, trudging alone with her sack. The children lay as still as stones; they could hear her grunting and muttering as she made her camp behind theirs.

Soon she was quiet; soon the whole camp was quiet. There was only a murmur here and a choked snore there. Little red fires winked along the hillside. Very softly, first the boy and then Sarah Jane sat up.

'Sleep now,' said the old woman behind them. 'Sun comes up soon. You go then.'

The children lay down. They waited to hear the old woman murmur or snore; and while they waited they fell asleep. Then the boy woke with a jerk, and that woke Sarah Jane. They sat up.

'Blue Eyes and Blue Eyes, sleep,' said the old woman. 'No bad thing here.'

They lay down in shock, for they had not thought the stories could last so long or follow them so far, or that sleeping-fires might show the colour of eyes. But the old woman crooned the shock away till they slept again, and when next they woke the stars showed that morning was near.

'You restless,' said the old woman. 'I talk, you listen.'

She told them they must take her sack; it held a shirt and trousers for the boy and a gown for Sarah Jane. 'Wundi and Yago not need 'em.' They must wear these things when they came near the white people, or they would be caught and shut up in a house and no one could help them. 'Old days, old ways, all gone. White man boss now; only old gins know Blue Eyes. You cover up.'

She told them how to find the Big River by the tracks of the monsters of fire and steam that rushed about the country. She called them trains, and huffed and chuffed to make their noise; and the children remembered, and huffed and chuffed too. She told of the special roads that the trains ran on, roads made of slabs of wood and shining rails; she made little roads with sticks, to show. She said there were many of these roads.

'All along hills, you see 'em. Go this way, that way. You stay in hills. By and by hard hills finish, good hills come.'

The children nodded, remembering.

'All towns, all people,' the old woman warned them. 'Roads; trains. You stay in hills. You hear chuff-chuff, you see smoke come up; you watch sun-way.' She pointed east. 'By and by smoke come up sun-way, far over. Then you find train's road, go that way. Big River four-five days.'

She gave them pieces of bread from the sack, and then she gave them the sack. 'Sun come up. You go now.'

They buried their fires quickly and gathered their things. The boy stood very straight, and bent his head and said, 'Thank you, mother.' He had never called anyone mother before. Sarah Jane was too shy to do the same, but she kissed the old woman's cheek and whispered, 'Thank you.' They ran along the hillside and down into a gully, and were gone before the others had stirred.

'They were kind!' cried Sarah Jane when it was safe. 'They knew us and still they were kind!'

The boy looked obstinate. 'They didn't know us. They were kind because we had proper tools and tucker.'

'Fiddle-faddle! The old lady knew us, and *she* was kind.'

'She was old,' the boy retorted; and because

she was both old and kind he carried her sack instead of leaving it behind a rock.

At night, for a game, they tried on the clothes, tangling their fingers in buttons and strings they had long forgotten. The fire-lizard watched with little, beady eyes as old as time. The clothes were worn and mended, crumpled but clean. The gown had a tucked yoke fit for a lady, and frills of lace across the shoulders above the long sleeves. To Sarah Jane it was beautiful.

'You look right-down handsome,' she told the boy; and he strutted like a soldier in his shirt and long pants, but only for a little while. Neither could Sarah Jane wear the gown for long; it fell loosely and easily from the yoke to her bare, brown calves, but the sleeves and collar made her declare that it felt like being tied up in a parcel.

Yet they took the sack with them south through the hills, and sometimes tried on the clothes, partly because of the old woman's kindness and partly for fear of being shut up in a house. Here in the rugged, jumbled hills there were rocks and gullies to hide in if anyone came; later there would be many people and no rocks or gullies. Then they might need to hide in the clothes.

Watching the stars at night, Sarah Jane secretly longed for the sea and the towns. She longed for her people: perhaps they too might be kind. She longed for something alive and warm and happening, so that she could share in it and be part of it. In the hills there were only empty trails, as though everyone had gone away; and once a man hammering at rocks, and sometimes, from a high place, a glimpse of those meaningless poles.

'I am Sarah Jane Tranter,' she whispered to herself; but now, longing to share in the life of her people, for the first time she felt like a devil.

And then, one day, they climbed a steep slope to avoid a broken gully; and far away, south and west through a haze of dust or smoke, they saw a town and the sea's long arm.

Sarah Jane took a deep, deep breath. She made her devil's face, and tripped the boy and rolled him down the slope. Then she sat down on the old woman's sack and gazed at the sea; and when the boy had growled, 'Oh, S'Jane!' he perched on a rock and waited.

After that they often looked down at the sea, and saw big towns and little ones, and farms and crops and roads along the plain. They saw those rushing monsters of fire and steam; and the polished rails on which they ran, shining in the sun; and houses and riders and walkers and coaches.

'Do you want to go down?' said the boy.

'And wear our fine clothes in this heat?' scoffed Sarah Jane. She had turned shy, and did not mind watching from the hills.

Sometimes, from one high place and then another, they saw towns and houses being built, and roads made, and shining rails laid for the trains. And at last the barren hills ended in the foothills and valleys that led to the softer hills, and the children came among Sarah

Jane's people.

There were little towns set amid golden fields of wheat. They had churches, and schools out of which children swarmed like bees. Between the towns there were farmhouses built of dark stone. All the country seemed to have turned into farms; there were only the roads to walk on. Other people walked along them too, or rode horses, or drove carriages and drays. The children stared hard at Sarah Jane and the boy; the grown-ups looked frowningly and then looked away.

'You'll know me again,' muttered Sarah Jane, nose in the air.

The boy gave back frown for frown, but when they were passing a field of wheat he dragged Sarah Jane into it. Hidden by tall, rustling wheat, they opened the old woman's sack and took out the clothes. Sarah Jane's groping fingers felt a sharp prick: buried in the sack, the fire-lizard had bitten her.

They left it there and put on their clothes. The old woman had been right, for after that the people seemed hardly to see them. It was only uncomfortable walking in the sun, wrapped up like parcels in their clothes.

There were other problems. Food was growing all around them, but the fowlyards and gardens and fruit trees were tended by day and guarded by dogs at night. When there was no stream near, water had to be stolen from a well or a square iron tank. 'I declare, it's the same as the dry lands,' said Sarah Jane.

They treated it like the dry lands, resting by day in a clump of trees, or a wheatfield, or under a bridge, and walking early and late. It was quieter then, and easier to find food — or steal it from some field where a farmhouse and dogs were not too near.

'What does a fire-lizard eat?' asked Sarah Jane, taking care not to crush it while she rolled a stolen turnip into the sack.

'Fire, might be. It comes out in the night and feeds itself.'

They were walking at dawn when they found the rabbits, on a rough hillside one misty morning when there was no farm near. They knew them as soon as they saw them, for there were rabbits in the settlements beside the eastern sea, brought from England for food. It took longer to remember what they were called.

'Rabbits,' whispered Sarah Jane after a few tries. 'By rights they should be in cages, looked after and fed.'

But the rabbits were feeding themselves, nibbling young shoots. They were smaller and greyer than those in the east, and they lived in holes in the ground. The boy killed one with his throwing-stick, and it was as good as a possum.

It was in the low country between the hills that they first came on a track with heavy timbers laid across it and long metal rails, one on each side, snaking away over the timbers; and they knew it was a train's road.

'It goes east!' cried Sarah Jane. 'We should follow it!'

'Have sense, S'Jane,' growled the boy,

though he was just as excited. 'It goes east here, and might be in a little while it goes west. The old mother said we must see it a long way east, and not till we're in the hills.'

Sarah Jane was disappointed and poked out her tongue and crossed her eyes; but the boy was disappointed too, and they walked all day by the road and camped near it at night, hoping to see a train. None came. They had to turn away to the hills.

As the ridges lifted them higher, the farms and little towns were not so close together. The roads grew long and lonely, and some-times the children could walk in the forest and carry their grand clothes in the old woman's sack. The fire-lizard gave up hiding in the sack, and visited the cooking-fire in its old way.

Now there were glimpses of the sea to the west; of towns so big that they spread along the plain; of trains rushing by under clouds of steam and smoke, shrieking like devils but too far off to be properly seen. It was wonderful to look down at night and see the coast patterned with lights, and the long beam of a lighthouse probing across the sea.

There came a night when they camped in a high place above a town dressed out in lights, and on the dark western sea even the ships were bright. The red, leaping light of little fires sprang up here and there; and suddenly, magically, there were coloured lights, very bright, springing into the air, and sometimes a noise like guns firing. The boy shut his eyes and began to chant magic words, and Sarah Jane seized his ankle in case he ran away.

'Fireworks! Don't be afraid, it's fireworks! It must be for the king's birthday or some other great thing! Oh, look!'

The boy would not look, so she told him how fireworks were made; and by then the scene was so splendid that Sarah Jane ran out of words and he had to look. The little fires were quiet, but a great fireworks show had begun on the ships.

Rockets leapt high in the air, and stars and

flowers of fire drifted slowly down. Bursts of coloured light exploded in the sky and threw their brilliance over the sea. There were animals made of lights: a lion and a hopping kangaroo. Giant numbers and letters sprang alight above the dark sea: 1901 FEDERATION. They had no meaning for Sarah Jane, but they made people very excited, leaping and waving around the little fires. She thought the long, unreadable word must be the name of the king. It marked the end of the show; but fireworks went on around the fires until the children fell asleep, and only the fire-lizard watched with old, bright eyes.

For a long time after that they talked about the fireworks: about what they had been for, and gunpowder, and kings. Even the boy grew interested, and tired of looking down from the hills.

'I wish we might creep through the streets while the people are asleep,' sighed Sarah Jane.

'And see a train close up,' said the boy. 'While *it's* asleep, might be.'

One day they were crossing a ridge towards another gully, listening as they went to the distant chuffing of a train. They heard its whistling shriek, and saw a drift of smoke above the hills — and suddenly they began to run. The sound of the train was growing louder.

'More smoke,' panted Sarah Jane, seeing another drift. 'We'll not cross the gully in time.' But when they could look down into the gully, they saw the train's own road snaking through it.

'East!' cried the boy, eyes flashing. 'It runs east!'

They climbed a little way down into the gully. Thick smoke bulged up from the trees on the opposite ridge. The train's whistle shrieked, very loud and near; it rumbled and snorted and panted like some great, angry beast.

'Not too far down!' shouted the boy, suddenly afraid. 'Stop, S'Jane. Wait here!'

They crouched on the slope and waited,

clinging to the stems of saplings. The train charged into sight, chuffing with smoke and hissing with steam, its inside glowing with the red light of fire. It sent a blast of wind down the gully ahead of it, and the long carriages and flat topped drays came swinging behind like the tail of the beast. It filled the gully with smoke and noise, and rushed by with a speed and power they had not seen from far off. Its whistle came back through the smoke, and it was gone.

'And people in it, too,' whispered Sarah Jane. 'Frightened for their lives, I don't doubt.'

The boy gazed eastward in a trance, seeing distant smoke rise over the trees. When the sound had died away, they climbed out of the gully and turned along its edge. A long plume of smoke rose between hills and drifted into the sky.

'We should go down again. Might be we'll lose the road.'

'Thank you for nothing. Another train might come.'

'We'll go down tomorrow. It's too late now.'

The gully ran steeply downhill, with the shining rails clinging to its farther side. When they looped the end of a bluff and vanished, the boy said it was time to camp. Tomorrow they would find the rails again, going east to the Big River.

While they slept, the fire-lizard came out of the grass and buried itself in the old woman's sack. It could brave fireworks and Hairy-Men and the Kuddi-Muckra, but not the train.

2

'Will it be towns all along the Big River, do you suppose?'

'Of course. Your people are like ants.'

'And ships with chimneys and big wheels?'

'Might be. I don't know, do I?'

Sarah Jane considered. 'There will be ships, for we saw them on the lake. It should be right-down lively.' It was exciting, after the long, lonely times; and under the excitement was the quiet flowing of the Big River itself, known for so long and glimpsed only once. She could feel that mighty meeting of rivers that flowed west across the land, and it swept away the dry lands and the vast lake of salt and the old, barren hills.

Here there were only marshes between the feet of the hills, and sparse woodlands of grey mallee, and the shining rails that ran east to the river. But sometimes a train came charging west or east along the rails, sending out signals of smoke; and the rails sang when it was coming and were hot when it had passed.

The children watched for these signs, and darted aside to the rough track that followed the lines, but they soon forgot to be afraid. The train was like a powerful beast on a chain: it ran only on its rails. It was exciting to stand near while it passed. Sarah Jane waved to the people in the carriages, but they did not seem to see. 'They've no time, so fast as it is,' she explained.

Once another figure appeared, rounding a bend in the lines: a bearded, blue-eyed man in shabby clothes, who plodded steadily on with his eyes on the track. A long, rolled up pack hung from his shoulders down his back, and he leaned forward a little balancing its weight. The children were not wearing their clothes and had no time to hide; they could only wait for him to pass.

The boy stood rigid, ready to run, but Sarah Jane felt shy and suddenly bobbed a scullery-maid's curtsy. It caught the man's eye; he glanced quickly and looked away, plodding steadily on. 'Charmed, I'm sure,' muttered Sarah Jane, nose in the air.

'Have sense, S'Jane. Do you *want* people to look!'

'A cat may look at a king, but it's manners to speak. We're not bandicoots, I'll have you know.'

The river pulled at Sarah Jane's feet, and just when they wanted to run the roofs and chimneys of a town appeared, straggled along the river's high bank. Hidden in their clothes, the children came near and looked down. They saw a wharf, and ships with chimneys and churning wheels, and long, loaded barges, and men lounging or working, and the lazy, brown water of the Big River. It came winding in from the east and curved away south.

The children watched from above, and whispered and pointed; it felt dangerous to be in a town. No one came near. A train whistled and came panting slowly in, grinding and clanking and hissing. It stood huge and near, with people stepping out as calm and untroubled as if they were coming from church. The children were entranced.

When they saw that no one noticed them they grew brave and walked right through the town, drank from a small, clear stream, and found an empty field to camp in. There they put their fine clothes away in the sack, and gathered firewood and lily-roots and quandongs; and at dusk the wild, grey rabbits came out of their burrows, and the boy took one with his throwing stick.

They built a shelter to hide their fire and ate while the dusk turned to dark. The windows of the town glowed with the golden light of candles, and the children felt as brave as young trees. The river and the town and the train were large in their minds. 'There'll be a night,' boasted Sarah Jane, 'when I'll creep near and look in the windows and hear the talk.'

'It's different now. You won't know it.'

'I can hear some of the words, being older, but I daresay they might fandangle a little native boy. You'd be better suited keeping by the fire.'

'Might be,' growled the boy. 'And then you'd never find your way back.'

They fell asleep watching the stars; hearing the chug and shudder of a ship going by, and the gruff voices of men on board; startled awake from time to time by the barking of dogs. After the long, quiet time it felt dangerous and exciting.

Early in the morning they began their journey up the river. It coiled and twisted through the mallee like a great, brown snake, so that the chugging and huffing of a riverboat would be near, then far away, then near again. At first the boy grumbled.

'We could walk across the loops in half the time.'

'The ship's near, and no need for hurry. Your grandfather's at rest, poor soul.'

They saw billets of wood heaped on the riverbank, and a man chopping branches to build the heap; and when the riverboat swept into view, it moored to load some of the wood for its fire. The children gazed in delight at its powerful, chunky shape, its shabbiness, the lofty wheelhouse and the great, dripping wheel.

'They don't notice us. We could get on.'

'Might be they'd notice then.'

They hardly ever noticed, though the children often stood watching because there was so much to see. There were coaches rocking by on the bank, and great pumps watering green crops on the hot, dry plains, and a man using bullocks and ropes to drag logs and tree-roots out of the river. He seemed to be looking straight at Sarah Jane, and suddenly she made her devil's face; but he only looked a little surprised and took no more notice.

When night came they had not travelled far, but it did not matter. There were trees to camp among, and fish in the river, and rabbits on the banks. In the morning they went on again with the river. They reached a little town and, since no one noticed, they wandered through it and looked and listened. They began to understand the strange way people talked.

The days went by, slipping like sand through the fingers, and it seemed that the river was their own. Sometimes it was hard to follow at all, for the way it turned and twisted and ran into itself, and for the new rivers that joined it. Sometimes the banks rose into high cliffs with birds nesting in them. Sometimes the old red gums spread their boughs wide over the water; and once, in a time of flood, the children spent a night in their branches.

Their clothes grew torn and muddy and were stuffed into a hollow tree. The riverboats were fewer and shabbier, but often there were trains; like the Magooya they had turned into friendly monsters, rushing north to the river and charging south again. Small, green farms were strung between the towns; and the children looked and listened, peeping through windows and whispering news to each other.

'They've only a great stove in the kitchen! The hearth's in the best room!'

'It's called a fireplace. She just said.'

'I declare! … The lamps are clever, so bright as they are. I've not seen a candle in a long time.'

Once or twice, in bad weather, they camped in the lee of some building, but it did not feel as safe as a clump of trees by the river. There the lights glowed only from a distance, and the fire was their own, and they were at home. No Hairy-Men or old spirits passed; perhaps the lights kept them away. But there came a night when new and different spirits drifted by.

At first the children dreamed: of loneliness, and searching for home. Then Sarah Jane woke and sat up quickly asking, 'Was it you called out?'

'Shush,' said the boy. 'Lie down.' He whispered to the fires, and fed them with sticks.

Moonlight had washed out the stars. Mist lay on the river, and ragged mist shapes drifted over the plains. Among them drifted other shapes, not seen but felt, like watching eyes. They looked and passed on, one and then another; the spirits of young men searching for home. The children felt them passing and lay still. They did not know that all the land was haunted on that night, but they felt it.

Soon they forgot, for suddenly there were magical things to see. There was a carriage without horses, carrying people, churring and banging along the road by some power of its own. People ran out of cottages to stare as it went by, and those in the carriage sat as proud as kings.

'I wonder they don't suck their thumbs,' scoffed Sarah Jane, 'so like a baby-carriage as it is.'

At night the light from windows shone white instead of yellow, and sometimes strange music rang out: more voices and instruments than a cottage could hold, all singing or playing together. The children, peeping in, saw that it came from a machine wound up with a handle. They learnt many new words on these visits, and the names of many new things. Sometimes a lot of people sat together in the dark, watching pictures made of light jump around on a white curtain. Towns were big, and so bright at night that they lay along the hills like patches of fallen stars.

It was in a town that the children heard a moaning in the sky. 'Is it a bad wind coming, do you suppose?'

The boy shook his head. 'It's too small.'

'It's never a bird. There's none goes on and on like that, with never a breath.'

'Of course not. It's some machine of your people.'

'A flying machine, I daresay!' scoffed Sarah Jane. 'What a tarradiddle!'

But the sound grew and filled the sky, and the boy seized her and dragged her under an awning, and the fire-lizard came and dived into the sack. The flying machine passed over, high in the blue sky, whining and moaning but sailing the air like a ship sailing the sea; and the town was alive with people staring and waving at the sky.

'I've no bones left,' said Sarah Jane when she could speak.

After that, the trains seemed like old friends from long ago. 'We could get on, like these others,' said the boy, as they stood on a platform watching people board the train. 'We could go somewhere fast and come back.'

Sarah Jane stared at him. When she could speak, she cried, 'Thank you kindly! And where will it take us, and how will we come back?'

But the boy's eyes were alight, for he had often dreamed of riding in a train. He said, 'It will take us to another place like this, so more people can get in. And we'll get out there, and wait until another train comes back. We'll get in that one, and get out again here.'

'But the people pay money, you've seen them! What will they say if we don't pay any money? It's only when we're quiet they don't notice. Sometimes they look and look away.'

'Oh, S'Jane! We'll be quiet, and we won't ride with the people. Come on.' He began to run along the train, away from the carriages where the people rode, down to a van where goods were carried. Sarah Jane ran after him, trying to argue quietly.

'What if it takes a long time and we've no food or water?'

He stood at the open door of the van, gazing at the wheels; acting quietly so that people would look away. There was no one near. He said, 'It won't. All the people have to eat and drink.' He stepped into the van and

Sarah Jane had to follow.

There were sacks and parcels, pieces of machinery and big, wooden boxes; and there was a seat for the man who rode in the van. It was easy to slip out of sight behind the boxes. 'We've not brought the fire-lizard,' grumbled Sarah Jane, groping in their own sack.

The man came in, closed and barred the door, and stood by an open shutter. The train whistled, shuddered, breathed heavily, and slowly began to move. The van jerked and clanged, and wheels groaned on rails. The boy's eyes shone, and Sarah Jane hardly breathed for excitement and fear. Neither of them dared to move.

The train puffed and panted, gathering speed. The wheels sang, the van rocked and swayed, the children clung to boxes that shook and trembled. Nothing terrible happened, and soon they grew used to the swaying speed and peeped over the boxes. The guard was sitting down and sorting strips of paper. Making signs to each other, the children crawled between boxes and packages to the open shutter and looked out, clinging to the sill.

At first they could hardly see, the flat country flew by so fast. But farther off it moved more slowly, and there a line of great, spreading gums went winding by. The children pointed and nodded: it was the river. There were low hills, flat and blue in the distance, slowly turning and showing new shapes. The boy watched them and frowned as he tried to remember.

Then the whole country slowed down because the train was slowing. Taking turns to lean out and look ahead, the children saw houses by a north-flowing stream. The whistle shrieked, and they crept quickly back to their corner. The man dragged packages to the door. 'We get out,' whispered the boy.

Puffing heavily, the train clanked and ground to a stop. The door opened; another man was waiting with a trolley. While he and the first man took packages from the van, the children slipped quietly past them and drifted down the platform.

'I'm shaken to a jelly! When will the train go back? Must we wait until tomorrow, do you suppose?'

'We won't go back. We'll find the river and go north. I saw the hills.'

'But we've left the fire-lizard! We've to take it back!'

'Oh, S'Jane! You know it always comes.'

'Fiddle-faddle!' cried Sarah Jane, stamping her foot on the platform. 'Just when I was grown used to the train.' A woman in a wide hat tied on with a scarf turned to look at her, and the boy's sharp elbow gave her a nudge.

'Shush. There'll be more trains, won't there?'

They went north and east, and camped that night on the river; and the Magooya, in the shape of a huge, red-eyed dingo, made threatening *cracks* to punish them for the train. 'I never!' cried Sarah Jane. 'So quick as it is to find us!'

Now they kept north as well as east, and the

plains slowly lifted to meet the hills. They crossed river after river and, when the sack had crumbled away, carried the fire-lizard over in the boy's hair. There were larger and lonelier farms where the dogs still took notice, but the people did not notice and the roads always took them past. There were roads everywhere.

'Where have the forests gone?' asked Sarah Jane.

The boy did not answer. He hardly remembered the time of the forests, but he missed them, for he knew how to live in them safely and well.

The days went spinning by as the eastern hills came near, and every day was full of wonders. There were women abroad in their shifts, with strange, naked hats on their heads; Sarah Jane laughed so hard that they noticed, and the children had to hide under a bridge. There were too many horseless carriages to count; they were called motorcars now, and did not look like baby carriages. They went by in a blast of wind, on smooth, black roads made by machines as big as a Magooya. Marching beside each road were the poles with wires. The country seemed tangled in wires.

Every day there were flying machines, like winged whales swimming over the sky. Once there was a great pond of water, behind a wall so immense that only a giant could build it. And at night, wide fields of fallen stars were spread over hillside or plain: the lights of towns too big to be real. The children kept away from them.

There were quiet roads to walk on, and narrow strips of forest left over from the farms and towns; but the forest foods and the little streams were gone. It was hard to find a good camp, or a bushrat or bandicoot or even a lizard to cook; and the fire-lizard hardly ever came. But Sarah Jane found water in taps, and often there were rabbits to catch and gardens to rob.

'It's thieving,' Sarah Jane would mutter, for her people seemed too busy to be kind and she remembered the gravy boat.

'Starve, then,' the boy would answer darkly.

'I've no mind to; only being older makes me think.'

'Have sense, S'Jane. What else should we eat? They've taken all the rest.'

Then she would fear that his golden scar looked pale, and would try to soothe him. 'Don't put yourself in a taking, then. The hills are near, so quiet as they are, and past them there's the sea.'

The plains swept up and up to the hills, till at last there were only low bluffs to be climbed. They were covered in ragged, ruined forest, tangled with blackberry, laced with morning glory whose pale flowers shone in the sun; but there were bush foods to find, and streams hidden under blackberry and fed by drains. The children toiled upwards, and found a road that ran east and north along a ridge. They followed it from within the forest as they had done before, and came again to heights above deep, blue hazes, and looked down on the eastern plain and the faraway sea.

3

'It's a right-down city!' cried Sarah Jane. 'Like that London where the king lives!'

If there had been wonders on the western plains, they were nothing to the wonders below. A strange kind of fungus covered the land and climbed into the hills; and as it came near, the children saw that it was the roofs of houses. Trees and gardens were squeezed between them, and tanks of water where children played; and here and there rose towers as tall as the hills, with rows and rows of windows glistening in the sun.

'How do people get to the top, so high as it is? It needs a day climbing stairs.'

'Flying machines, of course. The tops are flat, see.'

Flying machines droned over like bees, growing huge as they settled towards land. There were so many motorcars that they flowed like syrup and sometimes banged into each other. Trains without engines flashed along their rails, and a deep, dull roar rose into the hills.

'Do you want to go down and look?' asked the boy doggedly.

'I'd not take the fire-lizard down there!' cried Sarah Jane. 'We must look from here.' The city would surely terrify the fire-lizard, for in spite of wonder and excitement it terrified her.

'We'll keep west, then,' said the boy with relief.

That night they crouched on the heights with the stars pale above them and a world of brighter lights below. Long fields of lights ran away towards the sea, merging into a distant glow. Avenues of lights linked field to field, and rivers of lights flowed across dark places in between. There were red and green and blue and yellow lights, and lights that changed colour; lights that beamed and blinked and flashed; lights swimming across the sky as a plane sailed over. Sarah Jane was entranced.

'They'd not bother with fireworks. They've all the lights and colours they can do with. Can you find that Hill of Fire in all this change and fandangle?'

'They can't change the hills,' said the boy.

She was not sure he was right, for a string of lights was coming out of a hillside below like a rabbit from its burrow; and once there had been no burrows in the hills. For a moment the lights were gone and the stars were bright: it was a night long ago on heights farther north, when the boy cooked a wallaby while Sarah Jane searched the windy, forested dark for the light of a candle.

Then the lights shone again, and she knew that the boy was right. Forests had turned into cities, but the hills were still the same.

They built shelters and made a fire, and cooked a rabbit they had taken, and the fire-lizard came for warmth and safety.

There were quiet slopes to the west, and ragged forest where food could still be found.

There were streams still open to the sky, and roads that could be crossed if you listened and waited. The towns were small and old, and the valleys drew maps that the boy began to remember. But sometimes the slopes grew rugged and wild and drove them east again.

There the coastal cities came climbing up the ridges. It was hard to find a way through their streets, all alike and all in straight lines. They were filled with motors, now called cars, which might knock you down; and with people, who sometimes noticed if the children bumped into them.

The stores were so large and bright and busy that the boy was shy and would not go in. Sarah Jane went alone into one, and came safely out again by following close behind another shopper. There were little carts so that people could buy more; and the store sold some things and gave others away, putting them out in baskets for people to help themselves. Sarah Jane helped herself to a pink comb.

'Did you ever?' she cried gleefully, showing it to the boy. 'I had one once, do you mind? I wonder how I lost it?'

'The same way you'll lose that one, might be.'

The houses were small and close together, with small front gates opening into small front gardens; Sarah Jane called them poky, and complained that no one could drive a carriage, or even a motor, to their front doors. There were not many chimneys, but every roof had a small, wire shape fixed to it. To Sarah Jane these were perches for birds, but the boy believed they were devil-traps or some other magic.

'I doubt we'll ever find the sea again, so many streets and motors as there are,' said Sarah Jane sadly.

'Not here,' said the boy. 'Farther north.' But she thought he said it out of kindness.

Once they walked through a street at night, because then the cars were in sheds. Voices and music came from the houses, as they had heard before: the same voices and music in house after house, booming or whispering all along the street. Then, through a window, they saw one of the talking boxes: it had pictures to match the sounds, pictures as real as life and moving like life. It scared Sarah Jane, as well as the boy.

The people were easy to watch, and Sarah Jane watched them with awe. She had scarcely seen time passing while she wandered with the boy; she thought only that these were the people she had wept for at night, and that but for a gravy boat and a great white fish she might have been one of them.

They had changed a great deal since the Big River. They spoke loudly in short, sharp phrases, using few words and packing extra meanings into them. They liked fierce games, and seemed to quarrel even when they laughed. They wore strong, hard colours and an odd mix-up of clothes, and their hair was long or short, glued together in strips or sometimes shaved off. It was hard to tell males from females. The boy said they had no uncles or grandfathers.

'They just make up the laws they want.'

Sarah Jane crossed her eyes and stuck out her tongue. 'Fiddle-faddle! They *need* to be strong and fast, so dangerous as it is in these days. All of them crowded together with the cars and machines and streets: they need to be right-down brave!'

There were strange things to discover, even in the quiet hills beyond the cities: empty towers of steel, or trees lying uprooted and scattered by giants. Strangest of all, there were fields of broken earth where things were buried: clothes and cushions, broken chairs and boxes, rotting vegetables, rusting machines, torn books and papers, fish heads and carpets and old bones. It seemed that all the houses in a city had been emptied, their contents smashed and piled in a great heap for the machines to bury. There were flies and rats and sourness, and the children stared in wonder till the smell drove them away.

'Might be the people are dead, so their things get buried.'

Once they followed a track from the city's edge, west among trees, and camped above a deep, plunging gorge. Tall spires of rock stood over it, and far below lay the thread of a stream and the proud, spreading tops of a forest. When they had eaten, the children sat on rough sandstone and gazed into the gorge. It was full of moonlight and silence.

'It's kept to itself. It's what it was used to be.'

'They can't get in and cut it down. Too steep and rough.'

Sarah Jane was fighting her tangled hair with the new, pink comb. She paused and murmured, 'I wish …' But a plane moaned overhead, looking for the cities that spread east to the sea; and new hills were growing in the moonlight from the things that the brave, new people threw away; and the people were crowded in little rooms watching pictures that moved and spoke. How could one kitchen-maid wish them all away for the sake of a forest?

Later, in the safety and shelter of trees, the children lay half dreaming by their fires and the fire-lizard watched among the coals. The moon swung over the gorge, and shadows came climbing out of it.

They were Hairy-Men, with long arms dangling and round heads thrust forward. They saw the fires and crept near. The children and the fire-lizard lay still. The Hairy-Men grunted softly and made signs to each other. Then they crept off along the path through the trees. They had come to look down from the hills at the lights on the plain, to wonder at them and lay a dead lizard on a rock as a prayer for protection.

'Are you awake?' whispered Sarah Jane.

'Shush,' whispered the boy.

'They've gone. Only fancy them still so near!'

'Why not? There's forest still.'

But Sarah Jane could hardly believe it, for the Hairy-Men were shy and wild and secret.

How could they bear the cars and lights and the noisy, crowding people? The planes, and the great machines burying things? Sarah Jane herself felt lost and strange; though she had longed to see it all she could not grasp it. The Hairy-Men too must be right-down brave. Perhaps, in these times, all people must be brave.

Time went by and the cities fell back to the plain, and the old, weathered ridges spread west as well as north. The boy read the hilltops and streams, and the maps in his head, and turned more west. Beyond were wilder ridges dark with forest, but here there were easier hills and safer roads, thin forest and more foods. The towns were few and small.

The children camped on a slope at dusk, watching lights flower in a town below; and Sarah Jane asked, 'What would that be, do you suppose?'

'What would *what* be?'

'How can I say when it's the very thing I'm asking? See, it's white, and hung in the air.

Look, now! It's lit up!'

A beam of light had cut across the dusk to a white surface, and on it giant pictures moved. Rows of cars stood below in the dusk, and more came with dimmed lights. They looked small because the pictures were so big. A beach big enough to walk on hung in the air while the waves broke and washed along it. There were people bigger than life; sometimes their faces filled the screen, bigger than the Magooya's shapes.

The boy rolled over and hid his face, whispering magic words.

'It's no more than pictures, like in the houses,' said Sarah Jane crossly; but after a while she lay down in her shelter and shut her eyes. The pictures went on and on, huge and bright and flat. Their colours shone through closed eyelids, and she hoped no Hairy-Men would see them.

It was not long afterwards that they looked down on a river, and the boy said it was the Magooya's.

'Are you certain sure?'

'Of course.'

'How can you tell, then?'

'By the hills, of course, and the way the valley goes, and where we are.'

'It makes no matter, I daresay. If it should be wrong, we've time enough to find it out.'

'Oh, S'Jane!'

Slowly they climbed down from the heights and into a tangle of rivers. There were steep, rugged hills blue against the sky, and sometimes even Sarah Jane knew their shapes. The boy threaded his way through lower hills from river to river, and new ridges came near. In time they camped on a slope above a tree-lined stream, looking across a flat. A black road ran round the feet of the opposite hills; and the boy, pointing with his chin, said, 'That's the Hill of Fire. Tomorrow you can wait here.'

'Indeed and I shan't,' said Sarah Jane roundly. 'I'll come with you to say goodbye and a thankyou to the Magooya.'

'Have sense, S'Jane. Fire will take you for

sure.'

'Fiddle-faddle. Fire can't take water. And never think of creeping away before the sun, for I'll only follow. And I daresay you might wish to borrow my comb.' She spoke sharply because she remembered Loo-Errn, and because they had reached the Hill of Fire and she could think of nowhere else to go.

He did not accept the comb, or rub himself with fat as he had for Loo-Errn. His first visit to fire had somehow been right, and he thought he should do everything the same.

They left their camp next morning at first light. There was no sign of the fire-lizard. They crossed the stream where the boy had crossed before, and walked over the flats and the narrow, black road, and climbed the hill, circling to its hidden side.

No smoke hung there. They saw the blackened ground where long ago fire had come, and the tumbled rocks where it had entered the hill, and the baked cracks where the boy had lain and looked into its home. He lay there again and looked down: there was only darkness, and no warmth in the ground.

'Is it the wrong hill?' whispered Sarah Jane.

The boy sat up and shook his head. 'The fire's gone out.'

'It never has! This is its home, you said!'

'Not now,' said the boy heavily. 'It's gone. It's cold.'

'You can light it again! You have the power!'

'Have sense! No one lit it before, it came of itself. If I lit a fire it would be the same as a campfire.'

Sarah Jane sat down blindly. 'Then there's nothing. We've brought the Magooya traipsing over the land for nothing.'

'Might be it hasn't come,' said the boy, and laid his face on his knees. He had come a long way, through this long, changing time, to look into the darkness and see once more the golden eyes of fire; and they were lost. The sun, hidden behind the ridge, filled the sky with light; and suddenly the hilltop rang with sharp, warning sounds: *crack! crack-crack!* The

Magooya had come.

'Poor thing,' muttered Sarah Jane, 'so sad and angry as it must be. I've no heart for saying long words.'

The Magooya lit a cold fire all around them; red and gold flames leapt higher than trees. There came a long, sad howling, and a great golden dingo ran where the flames had been. All in a moment it swirled into smoke and rose towards the sky, looked down from large, pale eyes in a misty face, shrank into an old, bent man with no head, and grew wings and swept overhead as a giant bat. In another moment it squealed and reared, a black stallion with great, white teeth, and coiled itself into the monstrous snake Kuddi–Muckra, and leapt up again as an eagle with legs like young branches. The eagle swung down to the boy — and the fire-lizard was sitting on his shoulder. It scurried down his arm, skittered across Sarah Jane's feet, and darted into the cracked ground, the old home of fire.

The children ran to look, and saw only

darkness. Sarah Jane called into it. 'Goodbye to you, then, with your bites and frights, and maybe you'll bring back fire.'

'It won't. It's only a shape-changer.'

'It was happy, for all of that. It was like dancing.'

'Tonight you'll see it back in our camp.'

'I'd not come back if I found my home and my mam and dad, like I was used to have. Nor you if you found your grandfather. Or if we found the old forests again.'

'You said you didn't want them, you wanted the people and all. To be in it, you said, and not hiding like a devil.'

Sarah Jane crossed her eyes. 'I know that. I've seen it now.' She took up her digging-stick, and they followed the old trail of fire from the hilltop into the ridges.

'Where are we going? It's for you to choose.'

'To find a forest,' said the boy.

'I don't doubt they'll come and chop it down.'

'There's some too steep, where they can't get in. There's wild country east of here, and good hills running north.'

'And Hairy-Men living in them, I daresay.'

They camped that night high in the ridges, and no fire-lizard came to their fire. 'I said so,' Sarah Jane pointed out.

'Might be it knew there was fire deep down. Or why would it stay now, after all that time keeping with us?'

'The changes are too much for it, poor thing. Trains and cars and lights and streets and people. No peace and nowhere to go.'

'Oh, S'Jane! It's a Magooya!'

'And what's that? A tiny, little lizard! It's worse off than us, for there's two of us with nowhere to go.'

'You have,' said the boy heavily. 'You could go and live with your people.'

'And never grow up?' cried Sarah Jane. 'And if I could, they're not my people now — they're different! They've changed everything, and they don't even see us but for the dogs.'

She struggled for words, turning the ring on her finger. 'I'm not brave enough for them. We're out of our place. Boy ... will you stay with me till we find the sea?'

He looked sullen because of the tears on her face and because he knew what she asked; but he muttered, 'If you want to.' They looked at each other and looked away, knowing at last the pain that had grown, little by little, since the day they found a date carved into a tree.

'Don't trouble yourself,' said Sarah Jane gently. 'Living forever's not meant. There's my ring loose; and your scar, so pale as it is. It's from choosing, like the Fish Woman said.'

A soft glow had been filling the eastern sky, and now the moon rose, making black lace of the trees. It climbed higher, and flooded the sky and washed out the stars; and with it came a long note of music that poured like the sea and rang like a bell. It was the voice of the Great Ancestor.

4

The children sprang up. Then, for a time, they could not move at all. They only listened, and saw in their minds a wide surface of salt, and a shining patch of water that walked about, and above it a hole in a broken bank.

The moon moved higher. The singing stopped, and Sarah Jane whispered, '*Forever*.' She added wistfully, 'Only I can't remember it, so big as he made it … How do we hear him so far?'

'We don't,' growled the boy. 'Something's wrong. Someone's found him and brought him near.'

'Who'd have done that?'

'Not my people,' said the boy grimly.

They went back to the fire. The boy pushed sticks farther in, and the spurt of flame was reflected in his eyes.

'Must we take him back?' asked Sarah Jane.

'I doubt I've the strength for it.'

The boy sat frowning at the fire. He added another stick, making enough fire for two. At last he said, 'Now they know where, they could get him another time.'

She nodded. 'It's a safe place he needs.'

'In the sea?' he asked, with a sideways glance.

Sarah Jane tilted her chin. 'I daresay. It's his place.'

But the boy disliked this idea. 'Might be he came of himself and he wants to stay,' he argued.

'I doubt he'd do that. Indeed, when I think of it, I doubt he wants anything. It's only the stone and the singing that's here. *He's* in forever.'

'We don't know what he wants till we find him,' said the boy, and began to make the sleeping-fires. They lay by their fires and talked of the Ancestor, and what could have brought him east, and how to reach the singing, until they fell asleep.

At dawn they buried the fires and set out, finding grass-lily roots and ant's eggs to nibble as they went. To follow the singing they must head south again, across ridges and valleys towards the lonely heights. If they could camp in high places they might hear the Ancestor sing, and perhaps find him before the moon had waned.

'Keep hurrying, S'Jane.'

'There's a goanna went into those rocks.'

They paused to battle with the goanna, and to listen beside roads for cars, and to drink and cool off in a stream. That night they camped in the saddle of a hill and saw the lights of a town.

'Is that where the singing was, do you suppose?'

'I don't know, do I? We have to hear.'

The town's lights were strung across the dark like necklaces, far across a valley dotted with lighted windows. The children sat on rocks still warm from the sun and waited for the moon to rise.

'What could a person want with an old thing turned into stone? Taking it means he'd care for it; and then he'd not take it from its place.'

'There's bushrangers and those. They take without caring.'

The little windows in the valley shone brighter, and car lights flew along invisible roads. The town lay south-east, mapping with its lights a hill and a bend of a river.

'He'd not be there, with all its lights. He'd never see the moon.'

'Shush. It's coming.'

A silver blade rose above an eastern ridge. Slowly the moon rose, and in a moment the music came ringing across the dark. The children waited, listening, till the moon hung higher and the singing died.

'It could be the town,' said the boy. 'It's that way.'

'Fiddle-faddle. They've no use for an Ancestor there.'

For three days they travelled down the

valley between the twisted arms of the hills, and each night the moon rose later. In the valley the singing was lost. Only Hairy-Men heard it, where they clustered on hilltops; they thought it was the moon that sang. On the fourth day the children reached a town that climbed a hill on a bend of a river. They lingered outside it while cars flashed by in the streets.

'Is it the one we saw?'

'Of course. We should go up the hill while it's light.'

'And never mind the cars and dogs, I daresay, or if we've lost the Ancestor.'

'We won't know till we try. But if we have, there's that higher hill behind; we can go there tomorrow.'

They walked bravely over a bridge into the town, and trod pavements and turned corners into quiet streets. There were small shops selling cakes or books, bundles of wool, dusty vases and rocks. And there, in the late afternoon, they found the Great Ancestor.

The stone lay on a shelf behind the shop's window, between lacquered sea-shells and butterflies in glass cases. It was small and pale, and at first they did not see it because of the bright butterflies. Then Sarah Jane's eyes caught the glimmer of green and milky blue, and she saw the opal shape in the stone: the knotted cord like a backbone, and the fronds that had curled in an ancient sea.

Not believing it, she turned to the boy: his face was dark with anger, and sparks glinted in his eyes. She cried, 'No! We're not devils!' and walked blindly into the shop.

It was like being in a dream. The dark little shop was full of polished rocks and shells and woven grass bags and small skeletons. In front loomed a tall counter; behind was the window and the shelf where the Ancestor lay. Somewhere, someone was tapping with a hammer: there was an open door behind the counter.

Sarah Jane felt confused. The doorway darkened, and a man with a small hammer looked in. She smiled at him, but he only glanced around the shop and went away; so she turned to the window, picked up the Great Ancestor's stone and slipped it into her bag. Then she walked quietly outside, and out of the town with the boy.

As they crossed the bridge, Sarah Jane suddenly woke from her dream. 'Gracious goodness! What will the man do now?'

'I don't mind,' said the boy. 'I'm not there.'

'But it's thieving! There'll be sojers or these pleece!'

'Oh, S'Jane! It was thieving that brought him here. And they won't notice, will they?'

'They'll notice him gone! It's only a mercy they're not looking yet.'

'Shush!' said the boy. 'Listen, you: what else could we do? Tonight we'll put the stone in the moonlight, and then we'll know what's right. Now we'll go away down the river.'

They followed the river south until evening and camped under casuarinas. The town was only a glow behind a ridge. Sarah Jane caught a perch while the boy made a fire. The moon rose and the Ancestor sang, and the children remembered forever.

They could not speak of it because it was too big; yet it felt warm and comforting. Sarah Jane fingered the opal shape in the stone. 'If forever's a place for a small sea-thing ... so grand as it is, I'd not fear it. Would you?'

'Only for having to keep him safe.'

'He's safe enough! He could be in the shop, or we could leave him here, he'd not mind! It's only the stone; that and some trick in its making.'

'No,' said the boy, frowning in thought. 'It's not him, and it's not the stone. It's ... knowing ... and caring. Other stones don't have a picture of a Great Ancestor, and sing, and help people, do they? It's not for selling in a shop or carrying round in a bag. It's ... the land ... and knowing ... and people. It should be in a place where people can hear it.'

'There's no one hears it, only us.'

'We don't know, do we? Might be there's

others. We can try.'

They thought about it while they made sleeping-fires under the casuarinas and went to bed. The stone lay between them in Sarah Jane's bag, and after a while she spoke into the shadows.

'People in wild places, they must be. I doubt they'd hear him in towns and farms.'

The boy stirred. 'There's wild country we saw as we came. It was west; that's near south of here.'

Next day the river took them south; they travelled while the moon waned and grew dark and was new again. By then the river had become a creek cutting deep into sandstone. Steep-sided hills loomed over it, dark with forest, and the children left the creek to climb the ridges.

They climbed among smooth, grey trunks that soared upward like the masts of great ships. Plunging gorges opened into canyons, lined with rainforest and filled with blue haze.

'It's the old forest still!' cried Sarah Jane.

'But for the tracks,' said the boy; for there were narrow walking tracks, and wide tracks with wheel marks, and sometimes a bridge above a waterfall, and even wooden platforms for looking at the view. It was clear that people came there.

The children climbed slowly among the ridges and round the heads of waterfalls, wandering on, going nowhere. There were foods they had not eaten for a hundred years. Sarah Jane's ring grew firmer and the boy's scar brighter. They saw no people and heard only birds and the soft scuffles of fur; but at night, whenever stars glinted through the high roof of leaves and the moon shone in, they laid the Ancestor's stone in the moonlight and heard the strong, sweet singing.

'It's changed,' said Sarah Jane one night. 'It's not forever now.' She waited for the boy to say 'Have sense, S'Jane', but instead he spoke the words Loo-Errn had given him …

They were in some secret gorge. Forest grew around them, and mighty walls of rock rose to the sky. Water hushed and tumbled; moonlight glinted on it as it slid away among ferns. Children played there: hairy, round faced children who laughed and grunted softly. They were watched and cared for: a father rested after hunting, a mother crooned to a baby, a grandmother held out arms to take it. Their bodies were covered in red brown hair. The Ancestor sang and they seemed to listen; more of them came through trees and rocks to stand with dangling arms. They had old eyes, deep and knowing, set among wrinkles. They began to sing a soft, wild chant.

The moon was shadowed: the gorge and the people were lost. Sarah Jane wanted to cry, for she had seen a family in the kind of home she knew. But the Ancestor had stopped singing, and she and the boy were on the hilltop again — and the soft, wild chant was still going on.

There were real Hairy-Men. They stood around in a circle, chanting. The children were startled, but they knew the Ancestor's singing had brought both the dream and the real.

The boy took up the stone and held it out to the Hairy-Men. They stepped back, making soft grunts. They would not take it.

'What should we do?' said the boy.

Sarah Jane took the stone, put it into her bag and offered that. The Hairy-Men grunted again and waved their arms.

The children waited, helpless. Then two of the men stepped forward, scooped up the children and swung them high. The children gasped: each was sitting on a hairy shoulder, and from all around came a chorus of kindly grunts.

'It's words!' cried Sarah Jane between terror and hope.

'They knew!' cried the boy, clutching a leathery neck. 'They listened all those nights and followed us.'

'But why won't they take the stone, then?'

'It's magic. Might hurt them. It doesn't hurt us, so we're part of it. We're its Clever Men.'

'Fiddle-faddle,' said Sarah Jane.

And the Hairy-Men carried them off to the secret gorge, and hid the stone behind a waterfall, and cared for the children with their own. Perhaps they are there and still children; or perhaps they have chosen forever.

The Dry Country

The Salt Lake

The Great Ancestor

Hills

The Big River

The Train Ride

The Long Beach

The Goldfield

Cave where man encased in stone

The Boy's Fire

Loo-Errn's Country

Beach of Gems